PRAISE FOR WORKS OF JEREMY ROBINSON

"Rocket-boosted action, brilliant speculation, and the recreation of a horror out of the mythologic past, all seamlessly blend into a rollercoaster ride of suspense and adventure."
-- James Rollins, New York Times bestselling author of JAKE RANSOM AND THE SKULL KING'S SHADOW

"With THRESHOLD Jeremy Robinson goes pedal to the metal into very dark territory. Fast-paced, action-packed and wonderfully creepy! Highly recommended!"
--Jonathan Maberry, NY Times bestselling author of ROT & RUIN

"Jeremy Robinson is the next James Rollins"
-- Chris Kuzneski, NY Times bestselling author of THE SECRET CROWN

"If you like thrillers original, unpredictable and chock-full of action, you are going to love Jeremy Robinson..."
-- Stephen Coonts, NY Times bestselling author of DEEP BLACK: ARCTIC GOLD

"How do you find an original story idea in the crowded action-thriller genre? Two words: Jeremy Robinson."
-- Scott Sigler, NY Times Bestselling author of ANCESTOR

"There's nothing timid about Robinson as he drops his readers off the cliff without a parachute and somehow manages to catch us an inch or two from doom."
-- Jeff Long, New York Times bestselling author of THE DESCENT

THE LAST HUNTER

PURSUIT

(BOOK 2 OF THE ANTARKTOS SAGA)

JEREMY ROBINSON

OTHER NOVELS BY JEREMY ROBINSON

The Last Hunter - Descent
Insomnia
Threshold
Instinct
Pulse
Kronos
Antarktos Rising
Beneath
Raising the Past
The Didymus Contingency

For the real Solomon, my son and inspiration

ACKNOWLEDGEMENTS

I realized that I actually forgot to include acknowledgments with Book 1 of the series (if you haven't read Book 1, do yourself a favor and read it before continuing any further). Happily, I have the exact same people to thank this time around, so let's just count this for both books. That said, I'm going to make this brief.

Hilaree Robinson (my amazing wife) and Ed Parrot, you are fantastic first readers whose suggestions are always on target. Kane Gilmour, your edits continue to help my books shine. Stan Tremblay, your unwavering support is always needed and appreciated. My daughters, Aquila and Norah, your boundless energy and creativity are things even I aspire to. And Solomon, my son, I am dedicating each and every book in this series to you because I have never met someone so kind, giving, and loving. Without your example, The Last Hunter would not exist.

THE LAST HUNTER

PROLOGUE

Lieutenant Ninnis was once a proud man. An adventurer with a scruffy beard, blazing blue eyes and a swarthy disposition akin to a pirate—the nice sort. But that man died long ago. Or at least the parts of him that understood things like love, friendship…and forgiveness did. The latter of the three had vexed him for the past several months.

Little Ull, the hunter he had kidnapped, broken and trained, had turned against their masters. And a final conflict with the boy, whose memories of his life before Antarctica had returned, had left Ninnis wounded, inside and out. The pain from the broken arm and several snapped ribs paled in comparison to the shame that boiled his insides and kept sleep at bay.

As punishment for his failure to recapture the boy, Ninnis's wounds were left to heal naturally, over time, rather than accelerated by the blood of the masters. This not only heaped hot coals of disgrace on his head, but also kept him out of the ongoing hunt. No one knew Ull better than Ninnis, and without him, they would never find the boy. And if they did, they wouldn't stand a chance, not without the knowledge Ninnis possessed.

First, the boy had some kind of power over the elements. At first Ninnis had thought it was a side effect of being bonded with the body of Nephil, but Ull had always shown a strange resistance to the cold. Second, the boy's memory had returned. He knew he was really Solomon Ull Vincent, not simply Ull the hunter. So his choices and strategies would vary greatly from those of a typical hunter. And third, some part of Nephil did indeed reside in the boy. He'd heard it in the boy's voice when they last met. That made him unpredictable and more dangerous than Ninnis wanted to contemplate.

But none of this weighed as heavily on Ninnis's thoughts as the three simple words Ull had scratched into the stone wall. Ull could have left Ninnis for dead, having knocked him unconscious in the freezing Antarctic air. But he didn't. The boy had dragged Ninnis underground, laid him in a tunnel and left a message for him to find upon waking.

I forgive you.

Ninnis had scratched the message away, but it had been etched into his memory, haunting him every time he closed his eyes. After everything he had done to the boy—taken him from his family, starved him, broken him, stolen his memory and treated him like a dog—Ull had *forgiven* him? It didn't make sense. Even with the boy's memory returned, what kind of a person could do such a thing?

The strength of that gesture frightened Ninnis more than anything he'd faced before, but it also enraged him. He had little doubt that the message was left to taunt him. It made him look weak. Frail. Like an old man whose mind and actions were not his own. Poor, poor Ninnis.

It was time to set the record straight.

It was time to find Ull.

He would bring Ull back and break him again, or kill him.

Ninnis sat on a stool, checking over his equipment. Satisfied, he wrapped his belt around his skinny waist and tied it tight. He carried a water skin, binoculars, the trusty knife he'd had since his time in the British Army and an empty pouch for food rations he would hunt along the way.

Ninnis looked around his small room covered with symbolic graffiti left by the hunters who occupied this space during the thousands of years before his birth. After spending months recuperating here, he loathed the place. He was a hunter. Meant to roam the underground, to seek out and battle the enemies of his master—not to nurse wounds. He stood, walked to the door and yanked it open. A massive foot greeted him.

Ninnis stepped out of the room and looked up into the large eyes of a giant. He gave a bow and spoke his master's name with reverence. "Lord Enki."

"Rise, Ninnis," Enki said, his voice resonating in the tall hallway that held two rows of doors to the quarters of other human hunters and teachers. "You join the hunt?"

"If it pleases you, Master."

"It does," Enki replied. "You have handled your punishment with strength and character, as I knew you would."

"Thank you, Master."

Ninnis stepped back, surprised by Enki crouching before him. "I have something for you. A gift I think will come in useful." He held out a sword that glimmered in the flames illuminating the tunnel. It reminded Ninnis of a machete, but longer.

Ninnis took the offered blade and tested its weight in his hand. It felt good. Light. He swung the blade noticing how little effort it took. But it would not do. "Master," he said carefully, "It is a blade without comparison, but its size will slow my progress through the underground. I cannot use this."

"An assessment I knew you would make," Enki said with a nod. "But you are wrong."

The giant took the sword, pushed a small switch Ninnis had not noticed and gave it the tiniest of twitches. The blade curled in on itself, snapping into a tight roll of metal that would take up very little room.

Ninnis's eyes widened. A grin spread on his face.

Enki handed the sword back to him. "Test the blade," he said. "On my flesh." The giant held out his forearm. "The blood that spills is yours."

Sword in hand, Ninnis toggled the small switch back to its original position and shot his arm out towards Enki. The blade unfurled quickly as it arced through the air, fully extending as it passed by the master's arm. A two inch deep, ten inch long slice opened up on Enki's arm, but only a single drop of blood emerged before the wound healed.

"I will call it Strike," Ninnis said. "As it resembles the serpent."

When the drop fell, Ninnis reached out for it, and caught the purple fluid on the sword's blade. He brought the weapon up to his mouth, paused for a moment, and looked up at the giant. Enki gave a nod and Ninnis licked the blood from the blade.

A moment later, the old hunter fell to the stone floor clutching his stomach. The intense pain felt like a fire raging inside his body. But then, just as quickly as it began, the flames subsided. Ninnis stood, feeling stronger than he had in years, and when he looked up at his master again, a newfound malevolence had entered his eyes.

"Now go, my hunter. Find Ull and bring him back to us so that his body might be bonded with the soul of my father. Do anything it takes. Do you understand? *Anything.*"

Ninnis nodded. He did understand. There were laws in this kingdom, and even Enki, who ruled the warrior clan, was subject to them. But he had just given Ninnis permission to break them if need be. That meant Ninnis could kill anything or anyone that got in his way, whether another hunter, a watcher, a gatherer or even a warrior. Ninnis and all his fury were to be unleashed on the underworld for the first time. He smiled at his good fortune and thought, *Your forgiveness will be your undoing, Ull.*

I am coming.

1

It starts with a shriek. The hunt. High pitched wails follow. Breaking branches. The pounding of panicked feet. A squeal and then silence. I've grown so accustomed to the sounds that I can sleep through them; I know, because I sometimes discover kills I did not observe, which is rare, because here, in this massive cavern I now call home, I know *everything*.

The hunters are a pack—fourteen strong—of meat eating dinosaurs I call cresties, and not because they have clean teeth. A large boney crest rises up behind their yellow serpentine eyes, giving them an ominous appearance. At first I believed the crest was involved in attracting a mate, but since both the male and female cresties have crests, my assessment makes little sense. And it's the females that cause the real trouble. Not only are they the hunters, but they're also far larger than the males. The pack's leader, who stretches thirty feet from snout to tail and stands fifteen feet tall, is the only creature here that really poses any threat to me. She's built like a T-Rex, but more agile. She has razor sharp talons, teeth the size of butcher knives and the disposition of a—well, of a meat eating dinosaur, I suppose. She is constantly nipping the others and once eviscerated one of the males who mated with a lesser female. I suspect she is unloved by the others, but she is respected.

I named her Alice after the Allosaurus from *Land of the Lost*, one of my favorite TV shows before coming to Antarctica. I can't remember how long ago that was now. My brain tells me it was two years ago, but my body, weary from life a mile below ground, says it's been longer. But time works differently here. What feels like two years to me could have been five on the surface. Maybe more. But I'm fairly confident my two year estimation is close to the mark.

The hunt has ended. The herd of oversized subterranean, hairless, albino goats has stopped bleating and returned to their non-stop grazing, confident that the cresties have been satiated for the moment. I can't see them from my cliffside perch where not even Alice could reach me, but I can hear the sound of tearing flesh and breaking bones. Inside of twenty minutes there will be nothing left but a blood stain. The cresties eat everything, including bones and horns.

I roll over on my bed of palm fronds. The dry leaves crunch beneath me and I long for my bed back home. I turn my perfect memory to that place. The home in Maine. My second floor bedroom. The window next to my bed looked out into the backyard. I used to lie there during springtime rainstorms, feeling the water as it splashed through the screen window. It smelled of new grass and wet metal. A childhood scent. The memory breaks my heart and a tear drops from my eye.

I had promised myself I wouldn't cry while living in this new world, but I wasn't myself then. I was Ull the hunter, vessel of Nephil, Lord of the Nephilim. But before that, for most of my life, I was Solomon Ull Vincent, son of Mark and Beth, friend to Justin McCarthy and all around bookworm with a perfect memory. But I was born here on Antarctica. The first and only Antarctican. And that made me special. More special than *anyone* realized, even Ninnis, the man who stole me and brought me here.

I think of my parents. Of the night I was taken from them and dragged beneath the snow. I still feel the pain of losing them, my perfect memory repeating the events again and again, searching for a way things could have been different. But how could I have known that a race of half-human, half-demon monstrosities—the Nephilim—lived beneath the surface of Antarctica. How could I have known that these heroes of old, these men of renown, who used to pose as the polygamist gods of the ancient world, would know about my birth? How could I know about how their spirit entered me upon my birth or about how they wanted my body to house the soul of their leader Nephil, the first Nephilim, who is currently trapped in Tartarus in the depths of the earth?

I couldn't.

It's insane.

But it's my life.

I have to live with it, and the awful things I did as Ull. I know it's not all my fault. I was broken, beaten, starved and forced to do awful things to survive. In the end, my mind was not my own and the memories of my former life were masked by a haze of hatred and violence. I hunted. I killed. And I kidnapped Aimee Clark, the woman who welcomed me into the world at the moment of my birth. She is the wife of Merrill Clark, the man who named me, and the mother of Mirabelle Clark, their daughter—whose photo I carry with me at all times. Mira is my hope. I think of her every day and cling to her memory. Not only do I long to see her again—she brought out the best in me—but I wish to reunite her with her mother. I know the pain of losing a parent and my chest aches from the knowledge that I did that to her. *I* took Aimee. *I* brought her to the Nephilim. And I left her behind when I escaped.

After consuming the physical essence of Nephil—a partially congealed dollop of his blood—meant to strengthen my body so that it might contain the giant's soul, I ran. Being born on Antarctica filled me with the "spirit" or magic of the Nephilim, but it also bonded me to the continent, to the earth, air and water. They are mine to control, though I do not understand how, and the effort often drains my body. But I was able to use this ability to conceal my flight, filling the underground with a snowstorm. I escaped from the Nephilim citadel of Asgard, named for the city of the Norse gods, in dramatic form, killing the real Ull, son of Thor, son of Odin, and the giant who I called 'Master.' I ran far and deep and eventually came across this subterranean oasis.

I once was just a boy. I became a hunter. And now I...am the hunted.

Although none of the hunters have discovered me yet, I can

sense them out there. Searching. I am far too important to their cause—the destruction of the human race that cast them out so long ago. And the hunters will find me. Eventually. Until then, I'll build my strength, test my abilities and come up with a plan.

And the plan so far? I have no idea. But I'm central to their plot and without me, they're stuck. I know that's not enough. I'll eventually have to do more, not because I *want* to do more, but because I *can*. The honest truth is that I'm terrified. I'm afraid that I'll be caught, that Ninnis will break me again, that I'll become Ull once more. The idea of facing another Nephilim makes me sick to my stomach. While I have physically adapted to this harsh world, I am not cut out for it. I would like nothing more than to leave this place, find McMurdo Base and fly back to Maine and my parents. I could be home in a month. But no one else can fight the Nephilim. And then there's Aimee, held prisoner somewhere. I can't leave without her. And she won't leave until the Nephilim are defeated. And that's what scares me the most; knowing I'll one day have to face my fears, most likely before I'm ready, and against my will. Someday I'll have to face the darkness inside me, the ancient malevolence called Nephil that seeks to consume me. I'm almost certain I will lose.

My train of thought disturbs me, so I sit up and stretch. The cavern is bright, but not with morning light. It's always bright, lit from the small glowing crystals that cover the walls and ceiling. In other caves, like the pit in which I was broken, the crystals are spread out and twinkle like stars in the darkness. Here they're so tightly packed that the cave is lit like dusk on the surface.

The sounds of the feast have faded. The albino goat is no

doubt consumed. The cresties will take another before the day is through. It's a good thing the goats reproduce like rabbits and grow fast. Otherwise the cresties would have burned through the cavern's main food source long ago. I don't eat the goats. I tried once, but the cresties took exception and nearly killed me. If not for a sudden rainstorm—something these subterranean dinosaurs had never seen—Alice would have gotten me for sure.

I'm hungry and I search the perimeter for movement. The lake is one hundred yards to the left of my perch. It supplies me with fresh water and an abundance of fish, which has become my staple diet along with an assortment of mushrooms, leafy plants and the occasional oversized albino centipede. "All the nutrition a growing boy needs," I say.

I focus my eyes in the distance, searching the canopy of lush trees that somehow manage to grow green in this underground tropical Shangri-La, far away from the sun—a subterranean rainforest, sans the rain. Despite my genius intelligence and photographic memory, I have yet to figure out how this is possible and have chalked it up to being one more magical mystery that is the underworld. Trying to understand how grass, trees and flowers can grow green without photosynthesis from a scientific perspective is maddening. I gave up the task long ago.

Movement catches my eye. That's when I see her. Alice. Her head, shaped similarly to the large palm fronds, stands fifty feet away, her yellow eyes staring at me. Despite my being here for some time, she still sees me as an intruder. Perhaps it's because I escaped her wrath before, or maybe it's the scent of my hair. Originally a stark white blond, my shoulder length hair turned dark red, like the Nephilim's, as I was corrupted by them. A blond streak had emerged—some of my innocence recaptured—but for the most part, my hair is still blood red. And the scent of it, of the Nephilim in me, offends the cresties.

And there is Nephilim in me. The spirit of Antarctica. The physical body of Nephil. And I became one of their best hunters, serving under the Norse house. They transformed me into Ull, and while I was him, I reveled in their violent, mankind-hating culture. And a part of Ull still lives in me, calling for blood and for dominance. But far more frightening than that dark side of myself, is Nephil. His voice, buried deep, surfaces in my weakness and in my dreams. He is hunting for me, too.

Everyone is. "Including you," I say to Alice, letting her know I've seen her.

With a snort, Alice ducks back. I hear her feet pounding away. She prefers to ambush prey. And I'm pretty sure she realizes that's the only way she'd be able to kill me.

"Someday, Alice," I say, "you and I are going to have it out."

A distant roar responds. I don't know if she heard me or not, but I find humor in the moment, and allow myself an uncommon smile. Then I jump from my cliff-side hideaway and drop thirty feet to the ground.

2

A sudden wind kicks up just before I land, slowing my fall. Then I'm on the ground and running. Staying still in this cavern, other than on my perch, invites trouble. My scent is strong and easily tracked by the cresties, who have come to know it well. But they've just eaten and are no doubt lounging with full bellies.

Except for Alice. She never seems to rest.

But even she can't follow where I'm going.

Low hanging tree branches slap me as I pass. Brush clings to the leather clothing I wear. The best phrase I can think of to describe it is a loin cloth, but I find the term embarrassing, even in my own subconscious. If the kids at the high school I attended—several years ahead of time—saw me now, their teasing would never end. Not that it ever did, but it would be magnified to a scale I can't even comprehend.

Would it? I wonder?

My body is strong now. Athletic. I can kill (and have killed) dinosaurs. What would a few stupid jocks be to me?

Nothing! The voice of Ull shouts from inside me. *They would bow before me.*

Images of football players strung up and filleted fill my mind's eye. But these thoughts are not from Ull. He would simply run them through. I fought with the dark thoughts conjured by my imagination long before coming to Antarctica, but since taking in the body of Nephil, they've reached a new level of depravity.

The graphic images cause me to stumble for a moment. I pause, sucking in a deep breath. I'm growing accustomed to the images, and I'm sometimes able to push them away with thoughts of Mira, Aimee or my parents. When all else fails, I look at the photo.

I pull the Polaroid photo out of the watertight pouch I made for it and look at the two smiling faces. The first blond haired kid is me, sporting an uncommonly genuine smile. The second blond, with pouffy hair and dark skin is Mira. She's the first girl that took an interest in me, and we came close to kissing once, though it was accidental. Still, the sight of her squeezes my chest even after all this time.

The darkness fades and my thoughts clear. *I'm me*, I remind myself. *Solomon. Not Ull. Not Nephil. I am in control.*

I secure the photo back in its pouch and set out again, but I don't have to run for long. The lake is just ahead. I normally come here to fish these waters, but not today. Since arriving in this underground sanctuary, I have searched for a way out. The walls here are as solid as they are vast, and I have been unable to locate a single tunnel leading out. The only obvious exit is the one I came in through—the waterfall pouring into the lake from two hundred feet above. But even with the wind at my beck and call, I haven't been able to leap high enough nor scale the cavern's polished walls. I believed myself stuck in this place forever, until this morning.

The waterfall pours a continuous stream of water into the lake—thousands upon thousands of gallons every hour. But the water level never rises. And the air in the cave is far from humid. There is an exit beneath the water. I'm sure of it.

I just need to find it.

Which is easier said than done because the lake is nearly a mile long, half as wide and deeper than fifty feet (which is the deepest I've swum).

I plunge into the water and relax. Other than my perch, this is the safest place in the cavern. There are no large predators in the water—only fish. A mix of albino species I've never seen before and some ocean dwelling species, like Cod, that seem to have adapted to living in fresh water far below the Earth's surface. I kick out into the lake, hoping to feel the tug of a current. I never have before, but I wasn't paying attention until now. In the middle of the lake, I lay on my back and float, staring up at the crystal covered ceiling.

And…nothing.

Other than the small waves created by the water fall, my body is the only thing stirring the waters. *It must be deep*, I think. *Maybe too deep.*

I tread water again, laying out a mental search grid. I'll dive as deep as I can again and again until I find it. I wonder if I can use my abilities to aid the search—maybe create an air bubble around my head or propel myself through the water like I do through the air.

Twenty feet away, the surface of the lake ripples. The movement catches my full attention. The waterfall is far away. And I am the only thing in this lake that should be disturbing the surface. None of the fish grow over ten pounds, nor do they school. Which means something else—something large—is in the water with me. And I suddenly feel vulnerable.

I am confident on land, against cresties, Nephilim warriors and unknown dangers. I can hold my own with the best of them one on one. But I've never had to fight in the water; my movements will be slowed and my coordination will be thrown off by the need to stay afloat.

Don't back down, Ull says to me. *Fight!* And for once we agree. Fleeing is rarely the right choice in this underground realm. Turning your back on an enemy means certain death.

My weapon of choice is called Whipsnap. It's a shaft of highly flexible wood with a spear tip on one end and a spiked mace ball on the other. The original had a bone blade and a stone mace, but it was upgraded when Ull—*when I*—was accepted into the Nephilim ranks. I usually have it wrapped around my waist and clipped to my belt, ready to spring into action. However, the blade tip and mace make staying afloat a chore, so I've left it back at the perch.

That leaves me with my climbing claws. I made them myself, as well. Inspired by Justin's ninja magazines, the claws have three triangular, shark-like, "egg-monster" teeth on the palm-side that are great for climbing. On the knuckle-side are three spiked teeth that make convenient slashing and puncture weapons. Whatever side of my hand you get while I'm wearing them is going to hurt. I pull them from my hip-pack, slide them onto my hands and cinch the leather tight.

The water ripples again, this time just ten feet away. Whatever this thing is, it's showing no fear, which is typically a very bad sign. It means it's never had a reason to be afraid before; never known a reason to be wary.

Until now, Ull says.

Not now, I think back. *Let me focus.*

And he does, because in the heat of battle, he often surfaces as the dominant personality. Usually just for a few moments, but he is part of me. The part that hunts and kills—and takes pleasure in it.

Weapons in place, I let out a breath and slide beneath the surface.

The creature is large and only feet away. For a moment, I'm filled with dread. How can I fight something so big with just climbing claws? Then I see its black eyes and recognition slaps me in the face. We surface together, eyes locked.

He lets out a steamy breath that smells of fish. His way of saying "hello," I suppose.

"How did you get here?" I ask, not really expecting an answer. He is a Weddell seal after all. The creature's brown skin pocked with gray spots makes him nearly invisible under the water's surface. His ten foot length is imposing, but his upturned mouth makes him appear as though he's constantly smiling. But that's not why I let my guard down. I suspect this is the same Weddell seal that saved my life so long ago after I plunged over a different waterfall into an even bigger subterranean lake, bordering the ancient ruins of a city the Nephilim call New Jericho. My perfect memory scans every nuance of the seal's face and confirms my suspicion. This is the same seal!

The creature just stares, his whiskers twitching.

I sense he recognizes the claws as weapons, so I take them off and put them away. He moves closer and some part of me tenses. But I know this creature. He is the first and only thing I've met in this underground world that I trust.

"You need a name," I tell him, running through a list of options. He's a male. I can tell from the broad head and muzzle, which with seals, like with dogs, helps in identifying the males without getting personal. Dr. Clark would have named him something ancient, but given the number of ancient names already littering the underworld, from gods to cities, I scratch those options off the list. I decide to stick with my 1980s pop-culture references. This time I choose the *Herculoids*. "I'll call you Gloop."

The seal sniffs me and my hair, his whiskers tickling my skin and getting a laugh out of me. Then he moves back with three gentle twitches of his flippers, sliding away from me.

"Gloop, wait," I say. "Don't go."

And he doesn't. Instead, he turns to the side as the water all around us comes to life. A second Weddell seal surfaces. Then another and another. They keep on coming until fifteen seals, two of them pups, hover on the surface.

They dance around me, swirling through the water, spinning their large bodies in an act of play that is innocent and makes me smile. After a moment of watching, I join in, slipping through the water, twisting around the seals' bodies as they slide by mine. It is an elaborate dance with no leader, but when it ends I realize it had meaning. We are bonded. Like family. For some reason, these benign creatures, perhaps the only benign creatures in the underworld, have chosen to accept me.

Which is strange.

After seeing or smelling my red hair, most denizens of the underground flee or attack. But these creatures seem to see right past it, to my core, and they know I'm no threat to them. Ull would have been, but he's not in control right now. He's buried in my subconscious, pouting about not being able to kill anything.

With the dance done, all eyes are on me.

My mother sometimes referred to strange moments or coincidences as being "cosmic." I think she got that from the sixties. But for the first time in my life I feel the word makes sense. Because this *is* cosmic. I can feel these seals. Not just the pressure their bodies exert on the water around them—the water I'm bonded to—but I can feel them in my mind. In my soul. They're not speaking to me. Not like the Nephilim gatherers, who can communicate directly mind-to-mind. But I *sense* them. Their feelings. Their desires. And I understand, somehow, that they came here for me.

Why? I wonder. Then ask aloud, "Why?"

A distant shriek replies and I understand. The cresties are

hunting, but they've only just recently eaten which means—

A shout echoes in the chamber, feminine and angry.

I am not alone.

The others have found me.

The hunters are here.

3

I start for shore, but I'm blocked by several large bodies. The seals sense the danger and they want to keep me from it. But I can't leave Whipsnap behind. While I'm dangerous without it, I'm not at my best. If I don't retrieve my weapon I will regret it.

Gloop rises in front of me, pleading with his black eyes. I reach out and put my hand on his wet forehead, which is softer than I was expecting, and say, "I will be quick."

I can see he's not happy about it, despite the perpetual smile, but he slides beneath the surface and disappears. The others follow his lead and within seconds it's like they were never there.

I dig into the water, swimming for shore as fast as I can. I know I'm heading toward danger, but based on the human shouts—belonging to just one human female—and the multiple dinosaur shrieks, I think my enemies are preoccupied with each other for the moment. It's possible the hunters don't even know I'm here.

They will eventually. I can't mask my scent or the evidence

of my campfires after being here for so long. But if they don't know I'm here, or how to get out, I should be able to disappear long before they realize how close they came to finding me.

I move silently through the cave's jungle and reach the base of my perch moments later. Climbing the perch might expose me. It's thirty feet high. But I need to risk it. Leaving Whipsnap behind would be like severing a limb. I scale the wall quickly and then lay flat on top. I gather my few belongings, including the telescope Ninnis gave me for my last birthday, and take hold of Whipsnap. My plan is to roll off the perch and fall to the ground, but I can't help sneaking a peek at the action as the sounds of battle get louder. I turn toward the noise and find the combatants on a treeless grassy hill.

I see only one hunter. A scout. But there are fourteen cresties. Not even Ninnis, who is a master hunter and killer, could face those odds and survive. I might be able to escape such a fight—I *have* escaped such a fight—but I could never win. Strangely, this hunter doesn't back down.

The telescope extends between my hands. I put it to my eye and feel my gut tense. The hunter is a woman. She's dressed as I am, in minimal leathers to allow free movement through the sometimes tight confines of the underground; her white skin glistens with a sheen of sweat. I blink, taken aback by my response to her...femininity. I'd never been interested in girls before. Mira was the first to stir anything in me. But just the sight of this one has me feeling nervous.

I'm older, I think. Then I groan. *Puberty. Great. At least the Weddell seals won't comment if my voice cracks.*

I put the telescope to my eye again. The woman is fierce, fighting a younger, ten foot crestie, and winning. She leaps in the air and strikes the dinosaur on the head with a large stone hammer.

I've seen the weapon before. Many of the hunters, who are fully human and subservient to the half-human, half-demon Nephilim warriors, mimic their masters by dressing the same (as I once did) and by carrying a smaller version of their master's preferred weapon. In this case, the stone hammer favored by my former master's father, Thor. The woman's name is Kainda. She's Ninnis's daughter. And she has a serious reputation. Worse, I offended her by turning her down as my bride—not to mention a few more insults I heaped on top of that. She is a woman scorned and she's no doubt out for my blood more than any other hunter. It's not surprising she tracked me down first.

The young cresty falls beneath the hammer strike, its thick skull crushed. Five other cresties move in for the kill, but they're stopped by Alice's roar. Kainda has killed one of the pack and Alice wants revenge.

The pack parts and Alice pounds forward, pausing for a moment to sniff the air, maybe testing the scent of Kainda's red hair. Maybe searching for my presence.

Kainda, to her credit, stands her ground in the face of certain failure. Even the Nephilim think twice before taking on a fully grown cresty.

She wants to die fighting, I think. It is the Nephilim way. The hunter's way, too.

Kainda raises the hammer and charges.

Alice steps away, like she's surprised, but it's a feint. And Kainda falls for it.

The thick dinosaur tail whips through the air and strikes Kainda in the side, long before the woman has a chance to strike. She will not survive.

Alice, who has been my enemy for so long now, is about to help me without even knowing it.

I watch as Kainda pulls herself away, leaving a trail of grass matted down in her wake. Alice steps toward her, confident, but still wary. It will all be over in a minute.

Now's my chance. I slide the telescope into its pouch on my belt and leap from the ledge. The wind slows my fall, as always, and I run.

Away from the lake.

At first I don't even notice it, but when I do, I can't stop.

I'm headed toward the battle.

Toward thirteen meat-eating dinosaurs.

And I'm going to save her. Kainda. The woman who would love nothing more than to set my head upon the tip of a pike and roast me over an open flame.

I struggle with my sense of urgency. Could I really have feelings for a woman like this? What about Mira? My feelings for her have only magnified during my time down here. How is it possible that I've forgotten all of that? It's not.

That's when I realize these feelings don't belong to me. Well, not to all of me. They belong to Ull. In his eyes, Kainda is no doubt the perfect woman. The beautiful killer. Or do I just see something there I haven't yet realized? How much do Ull and I really share in common? It's all so confusing, so I decide to ignore the why and focus on the how.

I can't fight and kill all thirteen cresties, and a rainstorm might not frighten them off again.

Alice, I think. She's the key. Without her leadership the pack won't know what to do or whose lead to follow. I need to kill Alice.

The jungle clears, and I run up a knoll that leads to the battle. The high pitched shrieking that punctuates the climax of every hunt fills the air.

I reach the top of the knoll and leap. I imagine the cavern's air swooping up behind me and a moment later, it does. I'm carried high into the air, covering the distance between the knoll and Alice—nearly one hundred feet—in the blink of an eye. As I arc through the air, I see Alice opening her mouth to consume Kainda and I let out a war cry.

This time when Alice stumbles back, it's not a ruse. She was not expecting my approach, especially not from above. I grip Whipsnap, which is wrapped around my waist and attached to the belt, and I give it a yank. The weapon springs free, ready to stab, slice or bludgeon. A gust of wind bursts beneath me as I land in the grass between Kainda and Alice. A ten foot circle of grass bends away from my feet like an impact crater.

"Ull?" I hear Kainda's confused voice ask from behind me. When she realizes it's me, she shouts with a voice like some wrathful god, "Ull!"

She'd no doubt try to strangle me to death while Alice chewed us both to pieces, so I don't step any closer. But I shoot her a glance and say, "Kainda."

"What are you doing?" Her voice is filled with so much vitriol I think she's actually trying to kill me with it.

Alice's anger matches Kainda's. She roars at my sudden appearance. The sound shakes the air from my lungs and makes my head spin. If Alice knew this, she would have struck already. Luckily, the beast isn't that smart. She simply stands her ground, instinct guiding her as she sizes me up.

"What's it look like?" I ask. "I'm saving you."

"Why?" This question is the first that's not tinged with hatred.

I answer by looking back at her again. When our eyes meet, my stomach twists, and she must see this, or feel it too, because she looks shocked.

Before she can ask "why" again, a question to which I have no answer, Alice roars. I turn to face her, happy for the thirty foot long, several ton dinosaur that could devour the elephant in the room had it been a real elephant and a room instead of a giant cave.

Ull surfaces in that moment with a roar. Alice matches it. We charge to meet each other in combat, both knowing that one of us will soon lie dead.

4

Teeth snap above my head as I slide through the grass beneath Alice. She can't bend over fully to the ground without toppling forward, and I'm not about to actually collide with a creature whose left arm weighs the same as me. As the massive cresty matriarch stomps past, I thrust Whipsnap up, intending to eviscerate the beast. I'd be covered in blood and entrails, but it would end the fight.

Unfortunately, Alice's underbelly is shielded by thick, dense skin that Whipsnap's blade can't pierce. I leave a long scratch across her lower abdomen, but nothing more.

Alice wastes no time and follows her charge with a tail strike. The giant dinosaur manages to do this so quickly that I barely have time to jump up and over it. If not for the wind carrying me higher, I would have certainly been struck.

Of course, being hit by her tail is preferable to being eaten. Before I've landed, Alice lunges. Her jaws open wide to receive my small body. I land a moment before she arrives and throw

Whipsnap at her, accelerating the weapon with a gust of wind.

As Whipsnap enters her mouth, the jaws snap shut. For a moment I think the blade might have pierced the back of Alice's throat, perhaps even reached her brain. But then the beast yanks her head to the side and tosses Whipsnap away.

I slide on my climbing claws knowing that the blades are not long enough to do any real damage, but they're the only weapons I have left. Granted, I could rain hail down on the beast, but the effort would exhaust me. I'd be open to attack from the twelve other cresties, not to mention Kainda, who, while wounded, is no doubt still dangerous. I catch a glimpse of her sliding through the grass toward her hammer.

Alice charges. I match her again. But this time I leap. Her head drops down to meet me, and when her jaws open, I know her view is obstructed. She'll wait until she feels my body in her mouth before she clamps down. That's not going to happen this time, though. The wind carries me up and over her head, which passes just inches below me. I reach out with my clawed hands, find her neck and latch on.

The razor sharp teeth on my climbing claws bite into the skin of her neck. My body slams down as Alice rears up, but I wrap my legs around her and squeeze, locking my feet on the other side. I am stuck to her like a parasite.

Alice roars with a fury I have not yet heard from her, or any cresty before her. My presence, so close, disturbs her. For a moment, I wonder if she's as bad as I've made her out to be. Would she respond so violently to me were my scent and red hair not so tainted by the Nephilim corruption? There's no way to know.

What I do know is that if I don't kill her, she will kill me. And then the Nephilim will win for sure. Not that I've done anything to stop them. My incessant fear of facing them again has kept me prisoner here for so long already. *Why?* I wonder. I can face down a thirty foot dinosaur, but not the Nephilim. *What am I so afraid of?*

My pondering nearly gets me killed. Alice bucks like a rodeo bull and for a moment, my hands slip free. Snapping back to the problem at hand, I reach higher and stab my climbing claws into Alice's neck. I then loosen my legs and pull myself up. For fifteen seconds, while Alice flails about in an attempt to shake me off, I pull myself higher, toward her head and snapping jaws…and sensitive eyes.

Sensing my impending attack, Alice slams her head and neck into a tree. The tree falls, but not before knocking me senseless. I feel myself slip a little, but I tighten my grip before falling. Having felt my loosened grip, Alice repeats the technique, but misses the mark, slamming the tree over with her snout instead of my head.

As she lines up the next strike, I can see it will be more accurate. A voice shouts to me before I can brace for the impact.

"Ull!"

It's Kainda.

I look toward her and see her hammer flying through the air at me. For a moment I suspect she is trying to kill me, too, but the trajectory of the hammer's flight reveals otherwise. She is arming me. We are working together.

For the moment.

Alice begins her strike.

I let go with my feet, place them on the back of her neck, and leap.

Alice hammers the tree over and then looks about, no doubt wondering if she's knocked me free.

Above her, I catch the hammer. It weighs far more than I was expecting—*how on Earth can Kainda wield such a weapon*—but I put everything I have into controlling it. I line up my strike as I descend and put all of my strength into the blow.

The connection is solid. Stone and bone collide. The impact shakes my arms and the hammer falls free. But the damage is done. Alice falls limp, her skull crushed beneath the weight of Kainda's miniature replica of Thor's hammer, Mjöllnir.

I land in the grass next to the giant cresty, breathing heavily. Alice, however, doesn't breathe at all.

My enemy is dead.

I know I should cheer or shout some kind of victory whoop, but with the fight over, Ull's personality has gone missing. All that's left is Solomon. I place my hand on the giant's side and tears form in my eyes. She wanted nothing more than to kill me, but she was a force of nature. Killing her seems wrong somehow.

"You weep for your prey?" Kainda says, scoffing.

"I respected her," I say.

"She was a beast."

"And yet she was your better."

I look at Kainda, still lying in the grass. She glowers at me, but does not argue. She knows it is true. The cresty defeated her. If not for my intervention, Kainda would be dead.

"Her ilk may yet kill us both," Kainda says.

When the first of the remaining twelve cresties, a twenty foot male, steps around Alice's motionless form, I realize she might be right. The male is followed by the others, which form a partial ring around us. I could run. They've given me the opportunity. But it would mean leaving Kainda behind.

I'm tempted once again to leave and let the cresties solve that problem, but I can't have killed Alice for nothing. I am here to save Kainda's life, like it or not, and that's what I intend to do—

The male steps toward me.

—if I can.

I look for Whipsnap and find it twenty feet away. With a focused blast of air, I can bring the weapon back to me or send it flying into the neck of the male cresty. But I pause. Something about this cresty is different. Cresties shriek while hunting. They bare their teeth like wolves. They snip at each other in anticipation of the kill.

None of that is on display here.

The male steps slowly forward again, lowering its head. For a moment, I fear it will pounce, but then I see its eyes, turned down to the ground.

Subservient.

I hear Kainda gasp behind me. She sees it too.

I step toward the beast and its head lowers even further, hovering below my chest. We're only five feet apart now.

Do they fear me now? I wonder. Have I become the pack leader by killing Alice? It makes sense in a strange underworld kind of way, but I don't think that's what's going on. I think...I think

I'm being thanked.

During my time here I've watched Alice rule over this place like a ruthless despot. Everything, both prey and family alike, feared her. And now she's gone. The queen overthrown.

I step forward again and reach out a hand, placing it on the dinosaur's snout. It looks me in the eyes and I realize I have made several more friends today. "I'll call you...Grumpy," I say, naming the dinosaur for the Tyrannosaurus Rex in *Land of the Lost* that constantly fought with Alice the Allosaurus. "Go, enjoy your giant goats."

When I smile, Grumpy stands tall, lets out a roar and turns away. The pack charges into the jungle without looking back. When they're gone, I turn to Kainda and find her wide eyed and stunned. The expression makes her look human—kind even— and for a moment I get a glimpse of what Ull sees in her. But the spell is broken by her words.

"You have made a pact with our sworn enemies."

I laugh. It's a silly thing to say really, though I suppose not to someone who has never known anything outside of the harsh subterranean hunter culture. Realizing that Kainda has never known anything else, I picture her being broken as a child and steeped in a culture of hatred and combat. Had she grown up in the outside world, she might have been an artist or a songwriter. She might have worn pretty dresses and smelled flowers, and laughed. Really laughed.

But she didn't. She doesn't even know those things exist.

I pity her.

A single cautious step toward Kainda is all I'm allowed before she takes up a defensive posture. "I'm not going to hurt you," I say.

She doesn't trust me.

"I just saved your life."

Her face remains rigid, her hands bent into claws ready to strike.

"Fine," I say. "But I'm leaving you here." I point to the bluff that was my home for the past few months. "There is a ledge over there. Thirty feet up. You'll be safe there if you can reach it. You left a scent trail, yes? For the others to follow?"

She doesn't answer, but I know she did. "They'll find you sooner or later. Though it might take some time for you all to find the way out."

I pick up her hammer. Alice's blood drips from its surface. "But I don't think they'll attack you while you carry this." I toss the hammer to her and she catches it. She's confused by my kindness, most likely because she's never experienced anything like it before.

"Why are you doing this?" she asks.

I stare at her for a moment, asking myself the same question. Is it because she's beautiful and some part of me wants to be with her? Is it because she's Ninnis's daughter and I feel a lingering obligation to serve him? I determine it's neither of those things. The realization that these people have been corrupted by an evil beyond their comprehension breaks my heart. They are slaves who believe they are free. They're blind and they don't know what they're doing. Not really.

So like Ninnis before her, I have decided to forgive her. And

I tell her as much. "Because I forgive you."

"Forgive?"

She's never heard the word before. I quote the dictionary in response. "To grant pardon for or remission of an offense. To cease to feel resentment against an enemy." I add a personal touch, saying, "I choose to love someone despite all of the awful things they have done."

She whispers the word "love" to herself and looks down at the grass. I can see she's lost in thought, but part of me can't help wonder if she's trying to delay me so that the others might arrive before my escape.

I snatch up Whipsnap, enter the jungle and sprint for the lake before she even realizes I'm gone.

5

The waterfall that constantly flows into the cavern creates a steady breeze and carries scents down from the tunnel high above. I sometimes catch whiffs of creatures lurking high above, some known, some unknown. As I approach the lake and feel the waterfall's mist on my face, I smell something foreign.

I pause at the edge of the trees, testing the air like a dog, sniffing quickly. The scents are new, but without a doubt, human. The hunters are approaching. Judging by the number of different scents, there are six of them.

I look up and see nothing. They haven't reached the waterfall's edge yet. But they will soon. The hunters are most likely following Kainda's scent trail. Thanks to the flow of water and wind it generates, they won't get my scent until they've entered the cavern. When that happens, they'll smell me, Kainda and cresty blood. For a moment I fear they will assault the dinosaur pack, but no, with me so close, they won't waste the time. They'll give chase.

With Whipsnap attached to my belt, I run for the water. Gloop is there and barks at my approach, urging me faster. The seal can smell the hunters, too. I dive in, doing my best not to create a splash, and I swim out toward the rest of the pod. Apparently, I'm not fast enough for Gloop's liking. He gets under me and when I hold on to his neck, he puts his flippers to work and my speed through the water doubles.

As we get closer to the pod, they turn and head for the waterfall. The waterfall's roar fills my ears as we near it and I can now taste the hunters in my mouth. They must be standing in the water above us. I look up and see something I hadn't noticed before. A rope, dark and wet, dangles next to the falling water. This is how Kainda entered the chamber, and how the other hunters will soon follow. The pod reaches the waterfall before Gloop and me, and one by one they start slipping beneath the water. I sense we're going to follow and take three quick breaths. Then we're underwater. Not deep, maybe twenty feet. I look up and see the waterfall roiling the water. And then we're beyond it, sliding into darkness. We speed forward as strong flippers and a fast current accelerate our passage.

I'm blind now, which is a strange feeling, because I've grown accustomed to life underground. Then I remember that I've been living in a well lit cave for a long time. My eyes will have to adjust to the darkness again.

Spots emerge in the black and at first I think there must be glowing crystals or bioluminescent algae in this submerged tunnel, but when my chest begins to ache I realize that I'm close to losing consciousness. I tighten my grip on Gloop's neck and he seems to sense my panic. The water pulses past me as we push forward. The seal's back arches beneath me and our speed increases again.

Then we're free of the water. I gasp several times, sucking in fresh air.

I loosen my grip on Gloop's neck and give him a few gentle pats on his head. "Thank you, my friend."

The cavern is dark, lacking any sort of light. Happily, I haven't totally lost my night vision and I can make out the vague shape of the place. I'm still nearly blind, but at least I'm not immobilized.

I climb out of the shallows and onto a smooth, stone shore. The underground river flows past, curving through the small chamber and exiting through another tunnel. For a moment, I wonder if this is merely a pit stop for air, but the pod is already moving on, following the flow. Gloop slides away from me, staring into my eyes.

Then he glances beyond me. I turn and find a small tunnel, just big enough for me to crawl through. When I look back, my mammalian protector is gone.

"What's the rush?" I say aloud, but a scent carried on the water entering the chamber answers my question.

The hunters are still near. And if their scent has made it here, they have reached the lake. A dreadful thought occurs to me. I was stuck in that cavern for so long because the elusive exit was unknown to me. But the men and women hunting me have lived in the underworld for some time. They know these tunnels even better than the Nephilim, who are too large to fit. They won't have to look for the exit, they'll already know where it is! Not only that, they'll know where it leads, and if they are physically unable to follow through the water, they might very well know where this route will take me. They'll have no trouble escaping the chamber using the rope.

I dive for the small tunnel, slipping inside the tight crag and pulling myself through the Earth like a worm. I'm only one hundred feet in when I hear a disturbance in the water behind me. They're here! They've found me.

I move as quickly and quietly as I can. At this range, my scent is impossible to mask. They know I'm close. But I don't want them to know *how* close.

A scraping sound fills the tunnel behind me and I wonder why they're not trying mask their presence better. I test the air and smell only one distinct scent. Only one of the hunters is giving chase. The others must be searching the cavern while this one moved ahead, just in case. I glance back and see something sliding through the tunnel, moving like a snake. It's an amazing technique for moving through the underworld, and if I don't keep moving, I will be caught by this snake man long before I reach a larger tunnel where I can put my feet to good use.

After ten more minutes of scurrying through the small tunnel, I can hear my pursuer's breath behind me, each one a hiss as though he's determined to play the role of a snake. Just when I think he's close enough to reach out and snare my ankle, the tunnel opens up. I stand and sprint, confident that my stride can outmatch his slither.

When I hear the pads of his feet slapping the stone behind me, it's clear that he's also a faster runner than I am. He's going to catch me.

I focus on the air behind me and imagine it surging back. My hair billows around my head as a gust of wind surges past me, but does not affect me. The man behind me, however, is struck full force. I hear a grunt, and the sound of a body hitting stone. My defensive strike worked, but only momentarily. The sound of feet slipping on stone returns a moment later.

Hunters only give up when they're dead. Ninnis told me that once. But I don't kill people. Animals? Yes, though only for food or in self-defense. Nephilim? Absolutely. People? I can't do it. Not even in self-defense. It just feels...wrong. So I'll have to immobilize this hunter somehow.

The tunnel floor disappears beneath my feet and I fall forward. My instincts generate a gust of wind beneath me, and it saves my life. I twist my body around a large rib bone that would have skewered me if not for the wind, and I land on my feet.

Glowing crystals pock the cave wall, helping me see. I'm surrounded by bones, some larger than my entire body. There are cresty skulls, albino goat horns, and an assortment of limbs, and bodies, many of which I do not recognize. And most of them are large. I run around a pile of bones, looking for a way out and I'm faced with a cavern, the enormity of which I cannot fathom. It's like seeing the Grand Canyon in reverse. The floor stretches out past the horizon where I see what looks like white mountains. I take out my telescope as I run and take a peek.

The mountains are *bones*. They're everywhere, even beneath my feet, where I suspect the powdery white dust coating the floor is pulverized bone.

Before I can ponder this mystery I hear a rattle and grunt behind me, and I know that the hunter has lunged. I dive to the side, roll and yank Whipsnap from its place on my belt. My weapon twangs into place, clutched in both of my hands.

The hunter stands ten feet away, no weapon in sight. He's tall, at least seven feet. That's big for a hunter. But he's also incredibly lean. I look at his skin. He is pale, like me, like all hunters, but there is a strange sheen to his skin, almost reflective. His face is hidden behind a black veil that looks like it's actually been pinned to his forehead.

Hoping to get some hint of who I'm dealing with, I ask, "Who is your master?"

"I have no master."

No master? How can a hunter not have a master?

We circle each other. I feel Ull at the fringe of my consciousness, ready to take over when the attack is pressed. And I'm grateful for his presence.

"Why do you hide your face?" I ask.

"I am shunned."

He feints an attack and my blade keeps him at bay.

"You are a hunter?" I ask.

"No, but I will be when I bring you back."

"What are you now?"

"A tracker."

This creature being a tracker makes no sense. Hunters are expert trackers. We can sense things in the underground that no one else can. Our sense of sight isn't hampered by the dark. And we can hear and smell things few others can.

A bit of Ull emerges, scoffing at his claim. "How can you track better than a hunter?"

Because I can follow your thoughts.

The voice is in my head!

My foe reveals himself, pulling the veil up over his head. His face is white and noseless. In some ways he reminds me of a gatherer, egg shaped head, almond-shaped oversized eyes and a small slit for a mouth. But his eyes are not solid black, they're bright yellow with a black, cat-like slit for a pupil. That's when I see his skin for what it is—scales. White scales, which combined with the yellow eyes is similar to the seekers, a class of Nephilim closely related to gatherers.

Your escape route is admirable, Ull. Bold. The others will not follow you here. But you did not count on me. I am Xin and I will be your undoing.

A pressure builds in my head as he stares at me. It keeps me from pondering *why* the others won't follow me here. I push back, but find the effort far more painful. He's in my head, searching my thoughts.

His small lips turn up. I can hear him laughing in my head. *You are not Ull at all!*

He digs deeper.

Solomon? That is your name. Solomon Ull Vincent.

I see what he sees. My past replayed for his amusement. My youth. My parents. My kidnapping. Ninnis breaking me. Me saving Ninnis's life. Then Kainda's. But he has failed to see the only memory I fought to block: Aimee. If he learned about her, they would no doubt threaten her life to bring me in. And it would work.

So full of compassion. Your forgiveness is your weakness.

The pain bursts inside my head and I fall to one knee.

Xin charges.

I do the only thing I can. I let Ull loose.

6

With a scream, I charge forward bringing Whipsnap up to strike. I see my next five moves in advance. The first strike will open Xin's chest and put him on the defensive. The next three will cause him to stumble back, but won't connect, and then with a spin to conceal my action, I'll bend Whipsnap tight and release it so the mace connects solidly with his head. Seven seconds.

The first strike comes close to slicing open Xin's chest, but the wiry tracker is fast and flexible. Still, he is on the defensive, so I press forward. He avoids the next three blows, as expected, so I spin, bend Whipsnap and unleash the kinetic energy of the weapon, flinging the mace end toward Xin's head.

The blow misses.

Ull is stunned. He has never missed before.

What is *it?* I think.

A laugh sounds inside my mind. *I am half-human and half-seeker. An experiment of the thinkers and breeders—one of the few survivors. I possess the best of both species, but I am accepted by neither. But that will soon change.*

I thrust. Xin parries.

Whipsnap extends my reach much further than Xin's long arms, but I can't seem to strike the creature. I aim low, but he leaps. That's when I see it. He leapt *before* I swung. He leapt when I *thought* about aiming low. He's still in my head! He knows what I'll do as soon as I do it.

But why isn't he attacking?

Humiliation.

It was a rhetorical question! I shout in my head.

Stop thinking, Ull, I tell my other personality. *Stop thinking!*

My blows come fast and furious. There is no rhyme or reason to them. No technique. I'm like the kids fighting on the school yard, eyes clenched shut, fists swinging, hoping to connect. For a moment, it works, but I feel Xin's mental tendrils dig deeper and suddenly he's predicting what I'll do even before *I* know what I'll do. He's in my subconscious!

Get out, get out, get out!

Letting Ull lose was a good idea, but neither of you lack the mental will to keep me out. Xin's voice echoes in my thoughts. *Stop fighting and return to Asgard with me.*

I shout again, lunging, but he dodges every attack, bending his body, slipping out of my grasp. "Stand and fight!" I shout.

Very well, Xin says. His body bends to the side as I strike with Whipsnap. The blade is just inches from his ribs. Before I can withdraw my weapon and strike again, he sweeps his leg around and knocks me on my back. The hard stone floor knocks the wind out of me, but I've suffered worse. I leap back to my feet.

It doesn't take a genius to see that this is a losing battle, so I decide to use my other skills. Wind howls through the giant chamber.

Xin steps back, looking around us. He's confused. Unsure.

I focus on a nearby bone. A blunt femur from an unknown species. I will the wind to wrap around it. Carry it up. Strike Xin in the back of the head. The bone flies.

Xin tilts his head to the side. The motion is subtle, but causes the bone to miss. I turn my focus to the other bones lying around. He won't be able to dodge them all. But before I can lift the bones from the ground, I am struck in the face, which is confusing because Xin is still out of reach.

I glance down and see the femur resting at my feet.

I don't understand. The bone should have fallen when I turned my attention away from it. *Whack!* I'm struck again. A second bone clatters to the floor.

Such wasted potential, Xin thinks.

Not only does he know about my abilities, he's using them against me!

A cyclone builds around me, lifting me off the ground. Whipsnap flies from my grasp. The air is sucked from my lungs. I am trapped. A prisoner of my own abilities. Despite the whipping wind roaring in my ears, I can still hear Xin's voice as though he were speaking directly into my ear.

Your mind is different than others I've tasted. More complex. Layered. Ull is so like the other hunters. Primal. Arrogant. Strong willed. But then there is Solomon. You are weak and lack courage, but are so...full of information. Mathematical equations. Every sight and smell for each of your years. You have read and retained the words of Einstein, Shakespeare and...who's this? Dr. Merrill Clark.

He's close, I think.

And he hears my fear.

Close to what?

I fill my thoughts with images of Polaroid camera manuals. Page after page fills my thoughts. But then a conversation emerges. I'm in the car with my parents. With Mira. They're talking about Polaroid cameras and suddenly Mira is ribbing me with her elbow, asking me what I think. I focus on something else, but Xin has latched onto the memory. He plays it forward. Mira's head is on my shoulder. My heart pounds in my chest. She raises her camera and snaps a picture.

The picture.

He steps forward and reaches out a long, white scaly arm. He undoes the pouch where I hold the photo.

"Stop!" I shout. For a moment, the wind ebbs and my body lowered.

Ahh, he thinks. *Here is your strength.*

He reasserts his dominance over my mind and I'm lifted higher.

He laughs again. *How can this young thing mean so much to you? A hunter. The vessel of Nephil. And yet your connection to this girl, to this image, is far more intense.*

He's truly confused by my feelings for Mira. I can feel him sorting it out. Reliving my time with her. The intensity of my emotions overwhelms him. He steps back, shakes his head and contorts his face like he's just tasted something foul. The photo falls from his hand and he turns his full attention back to peeling back the layers of my mind.

He digs deeper than before, violating my most sacred thoughts. But none of them hold his interest like the two mental doors I have put in place. He knows these are my two deepest darkest secrets. They are the things that will unhinge me. Perhaps even break me. He knows this as surely as I do, but he can't see beyond my barricades.

He tests the first and senses my panic. *No, no, no,* I think.

But he doesn't fight. He moves to the second door and gives it a shove.

"NO!" I scream, panic sweeping through my body like a physical force.

This time he laughs aloud. I feel him pull his influence out of the rest of my mind and focus on that single mental barricade.

The wind falls away and I drop to the ground, clutching my head. "Don't," I say. "Please!"

The barricade weakens.

"Don't let him out!"

Xin has no intention of stopping. The idea of breaking me is too enticing. If he accomplished something the infamous Ninnis failed to do, he would be accepted. He would be exalted. Praised!

Time seems to slow as I realize that Xin has entered my mind so deeply that he has given me access to his as well.

I relive his youth. A blue liquid world I mistake for the ocean at first. But there are distorted figures around me, walking past, staring in at me with big black eyes. I'm in a tube. A glass chamber. And I've been *grown*. A table is cold beneath me. Lights shine in my face. Sharp pain traces over my body as incisions are made. The process is repeated again and again until everything they needed to know has been acquired. Then I'm cast aside to die. But I don't. I survive and they're impressed enough to let me live, feeding me scraps. But I listen and watch. I learn and plot. And I desire to be accepted. To be…

Loved.

The deep sense of longing brings tears to my eyes and removes the last bit of strength I have.

The barricade breaks.

Xin is the first to scream, first in my head and then in his body as his mind is forced from mine by someone more powerful than us both. The blunt pain in my head turns into an all consuming fire. My scream joins with Xin's. Our voices roll through the giant cavern, bouncing off the walls for miles. I fight for control of my mind and body, but I'm weakened by Xin's invasion and I find myself incapable of regaining control.

Nephil is free.

7

I laugh hysterically, though the voice is not mine. It's as though puberty has come and gone and my voice has been replaced by a booming baritone. More than that, the words that follow my laughter are cruel and mocking. The kind I heard all my life.

"You wish to be a hunter?" I shout as though it's the most absurd thing I've ever heard. "I don't even know what you are!" I laugh again, when Xin reels back from the words like he's been hit.

Whipsnap is somehow in my hand again. I don't remember picking it up. I watch as a spectator, while my body strikes. The blade strikes Xin's side. His scales provide a momentary resistance to the blade, but the razor edge cuts through when the weapon is drawn back and fresh blood spills.

Red blood, I notice.

Not purple, like the Nephilim.

The sight of it only sends me—Nephil—deeper into a rage.

"You see!" I shout. "You're an albino seeker with *human*

blood! An abomination! Your body should have been dashed on the rocks and used as food for the feeders."

Feeders are egg shaped Nephilim with stubby arms and legs, massive jaws, rows of shark-like teeth, and pounds of fatty flesh, which is the staple food of many Nephilim. It's a cannibalistic society, but the breeders hatch the feeders—what I call egg-monsters—on a regular schedule and if they are not destroyed, they become giants, consuming everything they come across. Ninnis once told me there were three of them living in the underworld. I have yet to meet them and hope I never do.

My sight goes black for a moment. The blindness scares me. But I can still feel myself moving. Fighting. Killing. But the sight of it has been hidden from me.

Because it would revolt me, I think. And in my revolt, I would gain strength. Nephil must be contained, but I lack the strength after Xin's assault. As I feel my true self fading, I reach out with my thoughts.

Xin.

Xin!

Who? I can't—Solomon. How? Xin's thoughts are broken. Distracted. He's under attack. *Help!*

To help you, you must help me, I think.

I feel the mace end of Whipsnap swing wide and connect with something solid, but soft. Xin screams within my mind.

Back to the door, Xin shouts. *Close it!*

I see myself at the door, which I hadn't visualized before. It's old, and wooden, but held together by metal beams. I think I should have imagined a bank vault, but the ancient door somehow seems more appropriate. Nephil deserves a dungeon so that's what I've conjured up. Xin appears next to me, uninjured and ready for battle. While the condition of his physical body is a mystery to me, I suspect his injuries are severe.

What do we do? I ask.

Force him back.

I look to the door. It's open, but Nephil is not here. *How?*

This is still your mind, Solomon. You are in control if you choose to be. Bring him to us.

I turn all of my attention on Nephil. He appears immediately—by choice, I realize. He wouldn't back down from a fight. But he looks nothing like I thought he would—thirty feet tall, blood red hair, multiple rows of sharp teeth. I thought he would look like the other Nephilim. Instead he appears as a black, shapeless mass. A living shadow.

Little Solomon believes he is a man, Nephil says with a laugh.

Ull appears by his side, staring at me defiantly. I forgot that despite his independent streak, Ull is a hunter at heart and wants to see Nephil rise. While Ull is handy on the battlefield—he cannot resist a fight and does not wish to be harmed—he is ultimately my enemy. *I* am my enemy.

Focus, Solomon! Xin says.

I no longer feel my body moving. The fight has moved to the realm of the mind and the fact that Xin is still here means he is alive on the outside.

A wind kicks up inside my thoughts. I direct it at Nephil and try to force him through the open door. But it flows through him like he's not there. Ull charges at me, arms outstretched, fingers hooked. He means to distract me while Nephil finishes taking control.

Xin meets him half way.

The combat between hunter and tracker is intense and brutal, but this is in my mind and no blood spills. The pain is all in the mind, and as Xin lands a solid kick to Ull's gut, I feel the pain as well.

How am I supposed to force Nephil back, when the person helping me is also hurting me? Then I remember, *this is my mind*. The physics of this world are mine to control, like the environment on the outside.

Xin, I think, *come back to me!*

After quickly striking Ull, which dazes me, too, Xin dives back, rolls and regains his feet by my side.

What do you intend to—

I don't give Xin time to finish his query because by the time he does, Nephil and Ull will have figured it out, too. I don't need to force Nephil back into the old door. I just need to make a new one. Raising my hands out to either side, the walls of my mind stretch out, wrapping around Nephil and Ull.

The blackness of Nephil swoops through the air, heading straight for me with a roar. Ull charges beside him, teeth gritted with anger, but eyes filled with fear. He realizes what's about to happen and it actually frightens him.

An open door, four feet wide and eight tall, is the only space left open.

Nephil is nearly upon me, but just moments before he passes the threshold, a door appears and slams shut. Unlike the old dungeon door I had conjured up before, this is a bank vault. The locks clank in place.

Nephil is contained.

Thanks to Xin. I look toward my mental projection of him and find him lying down. His face is twisted in pain. Flowing red blood from several wounds catches my attention. It's only then that I realize we are no longer in my mind and what I'm seeing is real.

Xin is dying at my feet.

"Go," he says with his mouth, not his mind. "Before it—"

He fades before finishing. I kneel down beside him and place my fingers to his throat. He is alive.

A new mental battle begins. I am faced once more with an enemy in need. But this time, Ull is not attracted to the enemy. In fact, the voice of Ull has been completely silenced, locked away with Nephil, behind a door that will not open again until I want it to. Of course, the spirit of Nephil I now contain is but a tiny fraction, carried over to me when I consumed his physical body. I have no doubt that the full spirit of Nephil, locked away in Tartarus, would have no trouble overwhelming me. But that is a challenge I hope to avoid indefinitely.

Xin, on the other hand, nearly killed me. If not for his mental prying I would have surely been captured. If he regains consciousness, who's to say he won't take control of me again? I feel more prepared for a mental attack now, but it's a risk. I also don't know much about his physiology. The Nephilim heal from wounds in seconds and Xin is half-Nephilim.

But perhaps that's just on the outside? I wonder. *His blood* is *red.*

I think about what I saw while reliving his past. The mocking and taunting. A lack of purpose. A craving for affection. For acceptance. He is an outcast, a pariah among his own kind. We are more alike than either of us would have ever admitted. But maybe now, after we've shared our minds, and experienced each other's pasts, desires and fears, he will see that we have much in common.

And if not? Will I kill him?

I wait for Ull to chime in with a resounding, yes! But his voice does not rise. And the matter is put to rest in record time. Xin is only half-human, but that's human enough for me. I cannot kill him. Of course, if he gives me trouble I won't have any problem knocking him unconscious and leaving him to fend for himself. A part of me knows that's what I should do now, but Xin believes my greatest weakness is my compassion.

I intend to prove him wrong.

I just hope it doesn't get me killed.

8

Carrying Xin's limp, seven foot tall body saps my energy. His wiry build holds more muscle than I would have guessed. By the time I get him to a tall mound of oversized bones, my legs burn. I slide him gently off my back and feel a slick ooze of blood left behind. I'll have to scrub hard to get his scent off of me. Of course, it might also come in handy in concealing my own scent.

The concept of covering my scent with another living thing's blood should repulse me, but it doesn't. For a moment, I wonder if Ull is back, but then I realize that it's just me. And I'm changing. How could I not?

I turn my full attention to the bones and see a large intact ribcage at the base of the pile. It's concealed within the pile, but also holding the mass of bones at bay, creating a boneless nook. By the looks of it, it belonged to a massive cresty, perhaps even larger than Alice. I shift a few bones out of the way, clearing a passage to the open space.

With the path clear, I hoist Xin up over my back again and

pull him inside. No one will be able to see our white bodies hidden inside the bone mountain, but anything with half a nose will sniff us out. Xin's bloody trail across the enormous chamber guarantees it. Of course, that's also part of the plan, because the first scavengers to follow a trail of blood are always the oversized albino centipedes. The creatures are numerous in the underground and are the staple food for many of the denizens here, but their cottage cheese flesh is also good for sealing wounds and fighting infection.

I lay Xin down on the stone floor, propping his head up on a loose bone. A sigh escapes his mouth as he settles down. I expect his eyes'll pop open and he'll slice into my mind, but he doesn't move. I can see his pulse thumping behind the flesh of his neck. Still alive.

After covering the passage into our hideaway with bones, I sit down and think about how much I miss things like couches. It's been so long since I was comfortable. Though I have to admit, the beds in Asgard, made from layers of egg-monster skins, can hold their own against the best memory foam. But out here, in the wilderness, on the run, the best I can hope for is to not have my throat slit while I sleep.

Thinking of sleep pulls on my eyelids. I don't think I've been awake for a full day, but since I last slept, I've battled Alice, nearly drowned, was chased through the underground and slugged it out with Xin, Ull and Nephil in my mind. My body is fairly well conditioned so I think it must be the mental battle that wore me out. Then I remember that Xin took control of my body and used my abilities, which taxes both body and mind. Add to that several adrenaline highs and crashes and it's no wonder I'm tired.

I sit up cross-legged, determined to not fall asleep. The risk is too great. Aside from Xin, there are countless dangers in the underworld that could be drawn by his blood. But my head is spinning now. I close my eyes to fight the rising nausea.

"Hey Schwartz," my father shouts.

A memory.

One of my favorites.

We're at the beach, scouring the rocky shore in search of tide pools. The sun is shining, warming my shirtless torso. Clouds roll past in the distance. The air smells of sea water but is tinged with the odor of grilling burgers.

Justin's head pops up from behind a large rock. He's wearing his tinted sports glasses, as usual. "I see your Schwartz is as big as mine."

I laugh.

"Justin, I swear," says my father, standing from his position nearer the breaking waves, "Can I call my son by his nickname just once without you saying that? Just once?"

"Not likely," Justin says.

My father looks at me.

"What?" I say with a shrug. "I'm not his mother."

My father grins and motions with his head for me to join him. "Found a good tide pool. Lots of crabs. A few shrimp, too. Water is nice and clear, so I'll get some good close-ups out of it."

I climb through the rocks carefully. It's not uncommon for me to go home from the beach with a fresh wound, if not several. My parents call me clumsy, but it's an understatement because I seem to walk into doorframes and slip down stairs just as often as I trip on rocks at the beach. But I make it to my father okay, and I grin at the size of the tide pool. It's the perfect contained ecosystem, at least for a few more hours, and it's mine to explore.

While my father takes photos, Justin and I explore every nook and cranny of the tidepool. No rock is left unturned, no shell left submerged.

"What are we up to?" Justin asks me, knowing that I'll have perfectly retained the number and name of each creature we've discovered.

I could give him the Latin names for the animals in this tide pool, but he hates that, so I keep it simple. "Five crabs, three shrimp, eleven hermit crabs, thirty two snails and too many barnacles to count." That last part is a lie. There are three hundred and seventy-two barnacles, but sooner or later, I think Justin will decide I'm too weird to be around.

"There you are," my mother says as she climbs over the rocks toward us. She's far more agile than me or my father, even with the four boxed lunches she's carrying. The scent of burgers and fries arrives a moment before she does. We eat in silence, enjoying the view and the sunshine. I eat the tin foil-wrapped dill pickle first, then the fries before they get cold, and then turn my attention to the burger. This is a perfect moment. The food. The view. The smells. The company. With a smile on my face, I bite into the burger and wince.

It tastes wrong.

I spit out the food in my mouth and bring the burger up for inspection. I peel open the bun, expecting to see a large flat cheeseburger patty covered in ketchup and pickles. Instead, I find a crab. One of its claws is missing, a casualty of my first bite.

I drop the burger and step back. The crab crawls from the burger, but then it's not a crab at all. It just keeps on coming. Shell and legs emerge from the burger bun in a never ending chain, just like a big...centipede.

I'm dreaming.

I'm dreaming!

Wake up! I shout at myself.

Wake—

"up!" I flail as I awake, flinging the centipede on my chest against the rib ceiling, where its shell cracks. It falls to the stone floor, cracking some more, oozing white now. I turn to Xin and find three more centipedes gathered around an open wound on his leg. I can hear the munching of their mandibles as they fight to chew past his tough scales.

Whipsnap sails through the air bludgeoning one of the centipedes. As the dying creature twists in on itself, writhing as death takes it, the remaining two scurry away and disappear into the mountain of bones. When I hear the tick, tick, tick of the centipedes' sharp feet fade to nothing, I stab the two dying creatures to put them out of their misery. In the past, when I was fully Ull, I amused myself by watching a mortally injured centipede writhe around for fifteen minutes. The sight now makes my stomach twist. I hate seeing things suffer.

Have since I was a kid. One of my mother's favorite stories about me is about how after my father did a poor job of stepping on a carpenter ant, I crouched down and watched it squirm around on the floor. The thing was broken, and oozing and appeared to be trying to straighten itself back out. I looked up at my mother, tears in my eyes (not uncommon for me at the time…or any time before Ull took control) and asked, "Do ants suffer?"

My father heard the question and joked, "Yes, now let him crawl back to his colony and tell them to stay out of my kitchen."

This didn't help any, but my mom understood. She knelt down next to me, shook her head sadly and then stepped on the ant again.

"Better?" she asked.

I nodded, and wiped my eyes. I've always had a hard time accepting the suffering of others, whether it is a person, an ant or Xin—a half-human, half-Nephilim, who nearly killed me.

After retrieving a small stone bowl from my pack, I crack open one of the centipedes and scoop a dollop of its white flesh into the bowl. Using the knobby end of a bone, I mix the stuff, crushing away the lumps. When it's the consistency of yogurt, I bring the fresh ointment to Xin. He has three wounds that need tending. I move from one wound to the next, prying them open with my fingers and filling the gap with the creamed centipede meat. While the meat on the inside will ward off infection, the outside will harden into a protective, flexible shell that will slowly dissolve as the wound stitches back together. I've never actually used the technique on myself, but I saw Ninnis do it once.

With all three wounds sealed, I sit back and wait. I've done what I can. Whether Xin lives or dies is now up to him. But I'll watch over him. Make sure the centipedes don't come back.

When he comes to, he might try to kill me again. It's a very real possibility. But until then, I'm his protector.

The ground shakes.

An earthquake, I think. Antarctica sits atop one big tectonic plate, but that doesn't mean the earth never shifts. With so much ice bearing down on the continent, the plate can actually shift up and down during times of rapid melting or freezing.

The earthquake repeats.

An aftershock?

Maybe, but the vibration felt stronger the second time.

When the ground shakes a third time I know this is not an earthquake. Something approaches. Something large.

Keeping Xin alive might be harder than I thought.

9

"Run."

The voice of Xin startles me and I flinch away from it. His eyes remain closed and I wonder for a moment if I'm hearing things. Then I see his tiny lips twitch.

"Run," he repeats.

The ground shakes. Xin's eyebrows turn up. The tremors have him worried. Which isn't good—it's hard to picture him being afraid of much—but it changes nothing. I'm committed to the task of protecting him. "I won't leave you."

His eyes blink open, yellow and serpentine, and he looks at me. "I tried to kill you," he says. "I took control of your body. Violated your mind."

"You're like me," I say.

He sighs and shakes his head. "I am nothing like you."

"You saw my thoughts," I say. "My past. You felt what I felt."

The ground shakes again. I keep thinking the thing is nearly upon us, but each tremor is more violent than the last and I'm starting to think this giant might still be a ways off.

Xin stays silent.

"I experienced your past, too," I say.

His eyes widen. He did not know our thoughts were shared simultaneously.

"We're both…broken," I say.

He stares at me with those yellow eyes, but I see no malice in them now. He turns away, staring at the ceiling of our bony hideaway. "It doesn't matter," he says. "It's going to kill us both."

I can see he's resigned to his fate. Whatever is coming, he has no doubt it will be the end of us. But that can't be true. I've killed cresties and even a Nephilim warrior—who are supposed to be unkillable. I control the very air, water and land of the continent. And Xin…not only is he a formidable tracker and fighter, but he can manipulate the mind as easily as I can the weather. What could we not face together?

The ground shakes so hard that the bones above us rattle and shift. If the ribs give way we'll be buried beneath a mountain of the dead.

"You know me, Xin. Perhaps better than anyone else. You've seen who I am and know I wouldn't lie."

He nods.

"You are a better hunter than any I've met," I tell him. "Far better than even Ninnis and Kainda, both of whom I have beaten in combat. And *you* beat *me*. Beat Ull. I have never faced a foe as dangerous as you. The Nephilim are fools for not realizing it."

"And yet it is a boy, Solomon, that has defeated me."

My face scrunches. I have no idea what he's talking about. I didn't beat him in combat. That was Nephil. And without Xin, I wouldn't have been able to contain that evil spirit, either. "It wasn't me who beat you."

"But it is," he says. "Because I cannot kill you now. I can't even bring you back alive."

Despite the question being absurd, I ask, "Why not?"

"Because you have shown me a different path."

Small bones drop through the giant ribcage as a thunderous boom sounds from just outside our shelter. Xin grunts and sits up.

"You shouldn't move," I say.

He grunts a wet laugh. "If we are to survive the next few minutes, we will both need to move. And quickly." He looks me in the eyes, deadly serious now. "Behemoth is here."

Behemoth? "What is it?"

"I saw in your mind that you call them egg-monsters. Ninnis once told you about what happens to them in the wild. The size to which they grow? Their insatiable appetites? Behemoth is one of the three. It guards the gates to Tartarus. And though its hearing is all but useless, it will soon sniff us out."

"Tartarus! We're near the gates?"

"Yes," he says. "They lie at the other end of this cavern, ten miles from here. That is the second reason the other hunters will not follow. They fear the gates will open and consume them."

"But you don't fear the gate?"

"It is hard to feel fear when losing your life means little," he says sadly.

"Then why do you look so afraid now?" I ask.

I think I see a small grin on his face. "Because you have given me a reason to fear losing my life," he says. "Hope."

The sound of loud sniffing surrounds us. I can actually feel a breeze float past me as the air is siphoned past us. There is no doubt Behemoth will soon discover us.

"How do we beat it?" I ask.

"The Nephilim have been building an army for the specific task of killing Behemoth, so they might one day access the gates of Tartarus—the day you are to be bonded with the spirit of Nephil. In fact, if word of you being here reaches them, they might bring that army to bear immediately with the hopes of performing the bonding ritual now."

A new sense of urgency fills my body. "Then we'll run."

"That's what I've been telling you," he says. "You might be able to hold it at bay with your considerable abilities, and I might be able to attack its mind. But not today. We are both weak. And achieving the task alone might kill us both, if we're not eaten. Running is our *only* choice."

He climbs to his feet, stooping under the six foot high ceiling. He's moving fast for someone I thought nearly dead.

He notes my attention and says, "My blood is red, like a human's, but I still heal quickly. A gift from the genetic tinkering of my creators."

The concept of being created rather than born makes me feel even more empathy for Xin. He has never known the love of a parent, the comfort of family or even the concept of having come from somewhere. He has no ancestors. No lineage. He's truly alone.

Bones rattle as something large digs into our hiding space. The creature is testing our fortifications. A vibration pulses through the air, shaking my body and making me feel nauseous.

"Time is short," Xin says. "We must go now."

"What's it doing?"

"Purring," he says. "Behemoth is known for playing with its food. We will suffer horribly before being devoured."

Lovely.

"Are you able to trust me?" he asks.

"Do I have a choice?"

He shakes his head, no. "Our only chance of escape is distraction. As soon as we move, it will lock on to us and give chase. We need to give it something else to chase first."

"A distraction."

"Yes." He points at the bones around us and I understand what he wants me to do. The effort will leave me taxed and my escape, and my survival, will be completely dependent on Xin, who nearly succeeded in killing me only hours ago.

The bones around us shake violently. The creature is coming. I close my eyes, focus on the air in the giant cavern and put my life in Xin's hands. There is a howl outside, but it is not from Behemoth. It is my wind, swirling around. I can feel the giant form of Behemoth standing in the way of my wind, slowing it down, and I have to push harder to build speed. With a shout, I pull the wind in, and then up.

My hair flies up as the strongest gust of wind I've ever generated slides beneath the bone mountain and lifts it high into the air.

A confused roar deafens me and shakes the walls of the cavern. I open my eyes. The bone shelter is gone and Xin is running toward me. He scoops me up with little effort and throws me over his shoulder. The wind is knocked from my lungs repeatedly as Xin runs, and I am too weak to stiffen my stomach muscles or even adjust myself. But I do manage to look up.

The bone mountain has shot a hundred feet in the air and has bloomed out like a mushroom cloud. But it's not nearly high enough to block Behemoth's vision. The monster stands one hundred and fifty feet tall. Its black bulbous eyes are the size of swimming pools. Its body is similar to the smaller egg-monsters—essentially egg shaped, mostly jaw and teeth, but the red clumps of hair growing from random spots on the creature's body are long—and moving. Like tentacles, they whip out and snatch bones from the air, snapping them in two.

The giant head is tilted to the side, like a dog thinking, as it watches the flying bones finish their arc through the air and begin falling back down. That's when it sees us. Something within the black eye nearest us shifts and I know we've been spotted.

Behemoth lets out a roar that shatters the cloud of bones before it and sends the shards flying away. One of them catches Xin in the shoulder and I hear him grunt, but he does not slow. Which is good, because Behemoth takes a step in our direction and cuts the distance between us in half. Rope-like strands of red hair shoot out in pursuit.

I try to shout a warning, but I don't have enough air in my lungs to even whisper. In fact, my vision is starting to fade.

The jolts of Xin's footfalls slow and I feel we're moving

downward, or perhaps he's crouching. I can't tell. But the deceleration allows the living hairs to gain and one of them launches toward my face. A surge of panic rips through me and a gust of wind strikes the hair to the side.

My life is saved for the moment. But the effort has taxed me beyond my limits. A fuzzy haze fills my vision and consciousness fades as a faint scent tickles my nose. The other hunters are near. Xin has betrayed me.

10

When I wake, I find myself tightly bound, unable to move. But I don't panic. I remember Ninnis's lesson. Reach out with your senses before revealing you are awake. Some predators in the underworld will wait for prey to open its eyes before attacking. They're either just mean or waiting for confirmation that their meal's heart still beats. Either way, it's often possible to smell and hear enemies before revealing you are awake.

I test the air, drawing in a slow breath through my nose. The most notable smell is Xin's blood. It covers my body, and his, but the scent smells fresh. Like he's bleeding now. Lingering behind the strong smell of Xin's blood is the distinct odor of three hunters. Two men and one woman. I sniff again. It's not Kainda. She's either still stuck on my perch or on her way back to Asgard for a Nephilim blood bath, which will quickly heal her wounds.

Loud laughter cuts through the air. The woman. "I told you not to go after him by yourself," she says, her tone mocking. "A thing like you is no match for Ull."

"And you followed him into Behemoth's den?" This is a man speaking. He sounds young. "I have always said you have half a brain, Xin. A hunter must think before he acts."

"I know," Xin says, his voice quiet and lacking confidence.

A loud slap of flesh on flesh makes me wince, but there is no reaction to my movement.

"Do not speak to me until I ask!" the man shouts. "You're lucky I don't throw you back to Behemoth for letting Ull escape."

"Next time, track him, and leave a trail," says the woman.

"Next time," a second man groans. "Will we never be free of him?"

"When we advance in rank," the woman says, "and for some of us that will be sooner than later."

One of the men laughs. The other does not. And without opening my eyes I get a sense of what is going on. The hunters are youths. Perhaps older than me. Maybe younger. But they are not yet full-fledged hunters and they have been partnered with Xin. It's likely he knows the subterranean realm better than they do, and is a far better tracker, hence their reliance on him leaving a trail.

But what stands out most is that they believe I have escaped! I open my eyes and find myself tucked into a curved alcove that hides my body from the hunters in the tunnel outside. I can see that I am covered in blood—Xin's, andfar more of it than before. He's masked my scent with his.

He must have reopened his wounds before putting me in here.

"Which way did he go?" the woman asks.

"Toward the gate," Xin answers. "He had no trouble eluding Behemoth. In fact, the pair seemed to be working together. I suspect the spirit of Nephil in him gives him power over the beast."

I hear a gasp, and I smile. He's building a mythology around me that these youth are buying like it's a 50% off sale. Word will spread and as my infamy grows, so will my enemy's fear of me. I could probably leap out and send them all running. But I resist the urge. I'm awake, but my body is exhausted.

"What should we do?" the second young man asks. "Go after him?"

"Riodon, you're as stupid as Xin," the woman says, giving me a name for one of the voices. "If Behemoth is with him, we cannot hope to take him without the masters."

"Even without Behemoth, you would not be able to best him," Xin says.

"*What* did you just say?" Riodan is angry. I can hear him stepping closer to Xin, no doubt raising his hand to strike.

"He finished his training in record time," Xin says quickly, "and knocked the crown from the master Ull's head during his second trial. He defeated Ninnis in his first. *Ninnis*! And you saw what he did to Kainda."

"She said her injuries came from the beast slain by her hammer," the woman says.

"She would say that, Preeg," Xin says. I have two names, now. The woman is Preeg. "How could she reach the creature's head to strike it down while her leg was broken?"

There's a silence in the tunnel so profound that I hold my

breath for fear of being heard.

"None of us is a match for Ull the hunter," Xin says. "All of us together could not subdue him."

Xin and I both know this is a lie. He could have taken me by himself. But I appreciate the pep talk.

"He is the best of us," Xin finishes. "We must go for help."

No one argues.

"Then why does he run?" one of the men asks.

"He's gone mad," says the woman. "Too weak for the blood of Nephil."

"I could handle it," Riodan says.

This gets a laugh from the other two.

Between laughs, Preeg says, "Pyke is twice the hunter you are, Riodan, and not even he would think of taking the blood of Nephil."

"Hey," says the man known as Pyke.

"It's true!" Preeg says.

"Whatever," Pyke says. "If we're going to get help, we need to do it now. If Ull is heading for the gate, the masters will want to know. Delivering that news might be enough to advance. At least for some of us."

"Shut up," Riodan says.

"Xin," Pyke says. "What's the fastest way to Asgard?"

"I'll take you myself, just as soon as my wounds heal."

"You'll take us now," Pyke commands.

I know Xin could fight back. He could probably wipe their minds clean and leave them a heap of human vegetables. But he somehow restrains himself, most likely reverting to a role his has played throughout his entire life. But he does not give me up. Some part of him is rebelling, learning to be more than his masters believe him to be.

I have found my first ally in this dark place. An outcast, like myself. Thanks to him, these hunters are miles off my trail despite being just feet away.

"Up," Preeg orders. I hear a slap and I think she's struck Xin again. "Lead the way."

I see four shadows pass by the entrance to my hiding spot. The last of the four pauses a moment, sniffing the air. Then he's gone. A more experienced hunter might have detected my lingering odor mixed with the strong scent of Xin's blood, but the focus of these three is more on themselves than on the world around them. If any of them pass just one of the tests, I'll be surprised.

Solomon.

It's Xin. He's in my head, but just at the surface. He knows I can hear him—it would be impossible not to, even if I was deaf—so he continues.

I'm sure you have pieced together what happened. I was lucky to hide you before they came upon me. The frightened pups were waiting at the fringe of Behemoths lair, afraid to come in range of its tendrils. It wasn't until they sensed my return to the tunnels that they came out of hiding. I have bought you some time. Pyke will take credit for the false information I have delivered, and even when it proves to be incorrect he will never admit that he had taken advice from one as low as me. Though...you have shown me that I am not as low as I once believed. As they still believe.

Will I see you again? I ask.

It would be better if you did not, Xin replies. *I nearly turned you over to them. You have changed me—shown me that there is more to life than I knew. I cannot deny this. But your world could never accept me as I am. This is my world. Where I was created to thrive. And my ambition remains. We part as allies now, but I cannot make promises for the future. I am part Nephilim. The blood of Nephil courses through my veins.*

My chest hurts. My enemy turned ally remains my enemy.

Thank you for accepting me, young hunter. You are the first. I will try not to forget it.

I know what he's telling me. When I was broken, I forgot everything about my former life. He's warning me that the same could happen to him, even without being broken. He *is* part Nephilim, after all, and whatever he's feeling now might quickly wear off.

I sense his presence fading as the distance between us increases.

What should I do next? I ask.

I cannot tell you that, Xin says. *It is better if I do not know your intentions. But whatever you decide, do not think like a hunter. That is what they are expecting. That is what will lead you to them. You are yourself now, Solomon. Think like you. Seek allies. The Nephilim have many enemies, even within their own ranks. One day you will face an army of warriors. Even you are not strong enough to stand against them alone. Now go. Run!*

With his last words, an image of the underworld and tunnels I didn't know existed fills my mind. It's a map—a path—leading up and away from this place.

Thank you, Xin, I think. But there is no reply. He's gone.

A sweeping sense of loneliness settles in on me, but I fight it. There is no time to waste. When news of my location reaches Asgard, an army will descend toward me. Ull would stay here. Set traps. And look forward to the killing. If they see Ull as a threat, they'll expect as much. But I'm not Ull. So the question is, what would *I* do?

I step from my hiding place and check over my gear. Everything is here. I thank Xin one more time in my head, hoping he can somehow still hear me, and then I head up. Toward the surface. Toward the sun.

And my past.

11

Following Xin's advice to run is easier said than done. My body is worn down and my mind cries for sleep. But I push forward, and upward, hoping to reach the surface before the hunters can organize a thorough search. Luckily for me, creating a fire line search party through the underground is impossible. This is a three dimensional world of crisscrossing tunnels and there aren't enough hunters to search them all. Granted, each hunter can sense what is in the tunnels around them without ever entering, but there should be several large gaps through which I can sneak.

But the beginning of my journey is several vertical miles from the surface. And if you count the many winding tunnels I have to walk through, some of which have no grade to speak of, it might be a thirty mile hike before I reach the surface. Perhaps more.

The fastest route is along the underground rivers. They flow at a steady downward grade and carry my scent away from the surface. Any hunters ahead won't smell me coming. But I still need to watch every step and keep an eye out for any hint of company. Not only are hunters searching for me, countless predators would love to make a meal of me.

Despite not being able to feel hot or cold, the thought of being eaten sends a chill through my body. I stop and steady myself on a stalactite. I hold my hand up. It's shaking. I'm terrified. This is not what a boy my age should be doing—evading heartless killers in the wild Antarctic subterranean. I should be at home, watching TV, playing videogames and thinking about parties. Well, I hate parties. Social gatherings have always vexed me. But that's what I'm *supposed* to be doing. Not this.

I crouch down, squeezing my hands, and notice my legs shaking as well. Fear creeps up on me, burrowing into my muscles, adding to their weakness. *I just want to go home*, I think.

Ull says nothing to fight back the fear and for a moment, I miss that part of me. I think about unlocking the vault door and letting him out. Ull could fight the fear. But I cannot let him free without Nephil following. I must do this alone.

Seek allies. I remember Xin's words. But how am I supposed to find allies when this world operates on a kill first, ask questions later policy?

During my brief stint on a soccer team, my coach tried to help me overcome fear. Every time someone kicked the ball in my direction, friend or foe, I clenched my eyes shut, raised my arms to my head and turned away. I was never hit with the ball, but I was terrified of it. The coach, who was a real Grizzly Adams type, got down on one knee, took me by the shoulders and said, "Solomon, sometimes you just need to take a few licks. Then you'll realize the pain isn't so bad."

I'd played dodge ball, the sport in which I was essentially a human target. I *had* felt the pain and it was the very reason I flinched away from soccer balls, which I might add, are much harder than dodge balls. That was my last day on the team. I quit, told my parents why and then we all went to Friendly's for sundaes.

I wish I could quit now. I wish someone would say, "I understand, Schwartz. Some people are better suited for slaying dinosaurs and fighting man-gods. How about a banana split?"

But all I hear is the running water trickling past my bare feet. I look down at my feet, glowing white beneath the surface of the water. I stand that way for a moment, breathing, collecting myself, trying my best to bury the fear.

But the fear has an ally. My foot turns pink. For a moment, it confuses me, but then the metallic scent of blood hits my nose. The river is full of it. Something has been killed upstream.

A cresty, I think. The cresties have very few enemies in this part of the underworld. In fact, there is only one predator that could kill the dinosaur here.

Hunters.

My heart thumps against my ribcage and pushes a roar of blood past my ears. The only side benefit to this adrenaline rush is that I no longer feel tired. But that does nothing to quell my fear. Ull would have charged ahead, defeated the hunter—perhaps hunters—and continued on his merry way. All I can think of is escape.

I run through the miles of cave systems that I've memorized. There is a small crevice twenty feet back. It leads to a good-sized side tunnel, which eventually merges with another river, following in the opposite direction for two miles before emptying into the giant lake at the border of New Jericho—the abandoned Nephilim city where I first encountered my former master, the Nephilim, Ull. I don't relish the idea of returning to that place, but I remember that Gloop and his pod have swum those waters in the past.

The thought of the seal pod brings a small measure of peace to my mind. I do have friends in the underworld. They're just not human…or very much good in a fight. I decide on my course of action and stand upright, intending to head back to the crevice.

A mistake.

Not the crevice, the standing upright. I was so blinded by my fear that I ignored my senses. Had I stopped to listen, or really smell, I would have realized the kill, and the hunter, were only thirty feet away. It's not until I hear a gasp that I realize I've been detected.

My head snaps back and meets the eyes of the hunter. He's young, perhaps around my age. His body is slender and strong, perfectly built for moving through the tunnel system. His hair is blood red, but cut short. He carries two daggers, both dripping with the blood of the ten foot, adolescent cresty at his feet.

His smell reaches me and I recognize it. "Riodan?"

"Who are you?" he asks. I remember that this is the one prone to rash decisions. He won't back down from a fight, even with the grand stories he's heard about me.

"Where is Preeg? Pyke?"

"They left me behind." He spits. "Traitors. Now who are you?"

Several options flash through my mind. I can turn and run. I've got a thirty foot lead and I know every single footfall I need to take between here and New Jericho. Riodan is most likely lost. I can tell him who I am and try to scare him into retreating, but he's unlikely to back down and even if he did, all of Xin's misinformation would be for nothing. The hunters would know I was not only moving away from the gates of Tartarus, but also headed toward the surface.

Seek allies.

He's young. Impressionable. And dislikes his comrades. Maybe...

"I am Sol—Ull. The hunter."

He stands motionless, staring at me, probably weighing his options the same way I am.

"You don't sound so tough."

He's right. I sound like myself. When Ull speaks it's at least an octave lower.

"Is it true?" he asks. "Has the blood of Nephil driven you mad?"

I can see him flexing his fists. He's definitely sizing me up.

"I'm not crazy," I say. "I want you to...join me."

"Join you?" The request has him off balance. He wasn't expecting an invitation. "To what end?"

Convincing someone that everything they have learned, that all of the fear they have been instilled with since birth, is a lie, can't be easy. I decide to keep him off balance with the bold truth. "My master, Ull, is dead."

The look of shock on his face tells me the news was covered up. "Dead—by my hand."

I've just verbally slapped him for a second time. "What?"

"The Nephilim are not our masters. You can be free. All hunters can be free. You just need to—"

His war cry saves my life. I see the knife coming at the last moment and duck its spinning blade. The thrown dagger sails into the river beyond, but I'm not yet out of danger. Riodan charges.

I see ten different ways to counter his attack. He's inexperienced and his dagger is no match for Whipsnap. But I'm gripped by fear and I resort to the same tactic I developed in high school. I run.

I reach the crevice and slide in. At first the rough stone grips my body, tugging my flesh as I slide through. But then it opens up and I'm running.

"Blasphemer!" Riodan shouts from behind as he squeezes into the crevice. He's thinner than me and makes better time. I really don't want to fight him, and it has nothing to do with my promise not to take human life, it's because I'm pretty sure he'll take mine.

12

I remember watching the Boston marathon on TV. Every year, my father, who runs every morning, would watch the event that takes twenty thousand runners through the suburbs of Boston, via twenty-six miles of hilly, curvy streets. The fastest runners finish in just over two hours. I would often think to myself, "Why would anyone need to run twenty-six miles at twelve miles-per-hour outside of being a foot messenger for the Roman army?"

I now have my answer—survival of the fittest in the Antarctic underworld. And while I don't need to run twenty-six miles (I hope), I *am* sprinting at something closer to twenty miles-per-hour. And my worn down body is feeling the strain.

Riodan, however, seems no worse for wear. He's still just thirty feet back, cursing at me in Sumerian and ready to slice my back open with that dagger of his.

I've twice resisted the urge to turn and stand my ground. It would be a major breakthrough for me, but I'm so unsure of myself without Ull's personality that I keep running. After several miles, my goal is only three hundred feet ahead—the length of a football field, which some of the kids from my former high school could cover in just ten seconds. I think I can do it in less now.

Three seconds later, I can hear the roar of the waterfall ahead. It is one of two that empties out into the New Jericho lake. I once fell from the other waterfall and was rescued by Gloop. It was the first time we met. But this time I won't be falling, I'll be jumping, and I won't need a seal to carry me to the shore. Not only can I survive the three hundred foot fall, but I'm a good swimmer now, too.

After two more seconds, I hear Riodan shout, "Coward!"

"Don't try to follow me," I shout back. "You won't survive the fall!"

Nine seconds. My feet leave the river's stone floor and I leap out over the waterfall. I turn as I fall and see Riodan stop at the top, shaking his blade at me. I turn myself around and dive face first toward the water below.

Using my perfected technique, I use the wind to slow my fall and plunge into the lake as though I'd only dropped twenty feet. I arch my back and curve through the water like a torpedo. I surface thirty feet from where I splashed down. I lie on my back and start kicking toward the shore, which is nearly a mile away. I see the waterfall above but not Riodan.

Where did he go? Any good hunter would have made a note of my direction and—

Splash!

Water plumes into the air. Something large has fallen. I want to believe Riodan rolled a boulder over the edge with the hopes of it landing on me, but I know better. The fool jumped. While I can look over the edge of a waterfall, estimate the distance to within ten feet and calculate the speed I'll reach before impact—in this case, eighty miles per hour—Riodan has no such skill. Hunters rely on instinct, and Riodan's are so immature that he believed he could survive the jump.

It occurs to me that seeing me make the jump might have fueled his decision. When he doesn't surface, I reverse direction and swim toward him. There's no sign of him at the impact site, so I duck beneath the water and search the murk for his form. I find it thirty feet down, slipping deeper.

I cut through the water, reach out and take hold of his forearm. The broken bones of his arm *bend* in my hand and I nearly let go. I manage to pull his body to the surface and tilt his head back. I've taken two CPR classes and remember the instructions perfectly. But after just one chest compression, I know my efforts will be useless.

Nearly all of his ribs are already broken. As are his limbs, and most likely his neck and back. Even if I were able to revive him, he would likely suffer a prolonged and agonizing death from infection.

I tread water for five minutes, holding him in my arms like he's my child. In death, with his features relaxed, I realize that's what he is. True, he's not much younger than I am, but I'm still a child, too. Neither of us should be here.

"I'm sorry," I say to the dead boy. "You deserved better."

With tears in my eyes, I slide my arms out from under his

body and watch him slip back beneath the surface of the lake. While I didn't physically kill Riodan, it still feels like his death could have been averted. If I had faced him, and immobilized him, he would have never chased me. If I had subdued him I might have actually been able to talk some sense into him.

But I chose to run. Someone has died because of my cowardice.

I want to promise myself it will never happen again. That I'll stand and fight. But I don't. I'm not Ull. Not a shred of him remains.

I lie back and kick for shore, unable to wipe the image of Riodan's dead face from my mind. It is an image that will haunt me for the rest of my life, however long, or short, that might be.

At least I'm not completely useless. Free from the chase and back in familiar territory, I regain my senses and apply some underworld wit to my situation. My face is barely above the water as I swim on my back. I'm able to breathe through my nose and leave a negligible wake behind me. I kick with my feet underwater, moving silently across the lake. A hunter would have to be looking directly at me through a spyglass to see me. And even then, I wouldn't look like anything more than one of the Weddell seals.

When I reach the shore without incident, I'm flooded with relief. I've been here before. I know the way to the surface. But I'm unsettled again when I look up and see the ruins of New Jericho.

From where I stand, nothing has changed. Twenty foot ruins of massive walls surround the city. One of several sixty foot gates remains standing. Beyond is a grotto of temples, bastilles and obelisks that dwarf the grandest human structures of the ancient world. A ziggurat stands at the center of it all, stretching up toward the ceiling. Half way up, you could stare Behemoth in the eye.

Maybe Behemoth destroyed the city? I wonder. Imagining the event brings a smile to my face. I miss watching Godzilla.

I cut through the city heading for the still standing gate where I first encountered the Nephilim, Ull, whose name I share. I'd never seen a Nephilim before and took him for a statue. He was larger than life and terrified me—terrified "little" Ull, whose personality was dominant at the time. I fled and his laughter chased me through the underworld. That same passage down which I fled will carry me from this city once more.

As I wander through the city, sniffing for the scent of hunters but smelling only dust, I look at its grand balustrades and wonder how much of human history was influenced by the Nephilim. I see bits of Eygptian and Mayan in the stone work. Despite the ruined state of them, the statues almost look Roman. I pass a black obelisk that looks like it belongs in St. Peter's Square and I stop in my tracks.

A thirty foot statue stands in an open courtyard.

But this statue isn't like the others. It's new.

My heart twitches for a beat. Maybe it's not a statue at all! But the hair is gray, not red. The whole thing is stone gray. As I approach the back side of the statue, I recognize its form and check it for life one more time. I stand still and silent for a full minute. When I'm finally satisfied that it will not spring to life and devour me, I wander around to the front of the statue and look up into the frozen face of my former master. He stands tall, looking out over the city, his trademark bow in his hand, a quiver of arrows on his back and a cresty skull over his head—the head through which that I stabbed one of those giant arrows.

An inscription at the base reads: *Here lies Ull, son of Thor, son of Odin. Beloved by Asgard, but devoted to New Jericho, his home, his charge, his resting place.*

The genuine sentiment of the inscription makes no impression on me. Instead, I focus on the first two words: *Here lies...*

I look down at the fresh, brown, stone cobbles beneath my feet and realize I am standing on Ull's grave. The thought of being close to that monster, even in death, is more than I can bear. I run from the city, hearing his laughter in my mind, feeling it as keenly as I did when I first encountered him.

When I reach the cavern wall outside the city and locate the crack through which I previously escaped, I dive inside. I wail with fear as I scramble to safety like a mouse burrowing away from a cat. Thirty feet inside the tight squeezing earth, I pause and weep.

Crybaby.

The word comes to me like a distant voice.

"Shut-up," I say.

Crybaby.

"Shut-up!"

With a gasp, my crying stops. The voice is gone now, but I suddenly recognize its source.

Ull. He's trying to escape.

13

Ull remains silent and I think he must have found strength in my weakness. Nephil is an intruder in my mind, but Ull is a part of me. Always has been. Given the right circumstances it's possible he could re-emerge on his own. *Strength*, I think. I need to get stronger, and not just physically.

I stop and lean against the smooth wall of a tunnel carved out by a stream that has long since dried up. A dull light shines down on me from a lone crystal buried in the ceiling. The waterproof pouch at my side opens with a tug. I find the photo inside and remove it. The sight of Mira's face renews my strength, but even her image can't really make me stronger, or less afraid. That needs to come from inside.

With my mood slightly improved, I put the Polaroid photo back in its pouch and continue on my journey. But I don't get far before realizing I need a break. I've already covered more miles than the Boston Marathon and all of it was uphill, never mind the swim and the two mile sprint. I suspect I've made it beyond the reach of the hunters who are most likely descending toward the gates of Tartarus.

Even still, I'll need someplace defensible. Someplace no one would think to look for me.

When I think of the perfect place, I say, "No…"

I can't go there, I think. *It's too—*

My thought process freezes. I expect Ull's voice to rise up again. Maybe call me another name. But the anger I feel toward my fear is my own. If I can't face something as simple as bad memories, I will never survive, let alone resist the Nephilim. I have to do this.

Doing my best to ignore my rising apprehension, I slide out of the side tunnel and follow the waters of the High River. I don't stop until I reach the alcove where Ninnis trained me, like I was a dog, to obey and trust him. I did what he said, believed everything he told me, and came to think of him as something close to a father. He gave me the chance to kill him. Put the knife in my hand. But I couldn't do it. Ninnis had become my world. The idea of taking a life still goes against everything I believe, but if I had to repeat that day, I might plunge the knife into his chest. Everything after that day, including Aimee's capture at my hands, could have been avoided.

But the Nephilim would still be here, I think, *plotting the demise of the human race.* I would have only been postponing the horrors to come. Now I have a chance to stop them. If I can overcome the all-consuming fear that has gripped me.

The alcove is just as I remember it—a semicircle of gray stone, perhaps twenty feet in diameter where it meets the river.

The only evidence of our having been here is the black ash ground into a divot in the floor. Ninnis cooked his food there. For a long time he made me watch him eat, giving me whatever scraps remained—sometimes just the marrow from bones. Later we ate together, him teaching me the ways of the hunter and me eagerly absorbing his every word.

Solomon was gone by then. I had become Ull. An impressionable Ull.

I wonder if Ull could have been different. If that buried personality had been taught something different, could it have been a force for good? Could it still?

I remember the awful things Ull has done and said. *It's impossible*, I think. Ull is just as much a monster as anything else living in this world.

The memories here are strong, and they've shaken loose some things I would prefer to forget, but I have not yet reached my destination. That lies through the tunnel at the far end of the alcove. It's not much more than a large crack in the stone wall, but it was Ull's birth canal, so to speak. When I entered the cavern on the other side, I was Solomon. When I came out, I was Ull.

Will the same thing happen if I go in again?

Be brave, I tell myself. *Face your fears.*

I crouch down by the tunnel. The space is small, but I've navigated smaller. I steel myself with a deep breath, and enter. I slide through the tunnel, using the handholds I remember from my exit, and make good time. I pause halfway through, looking at the tight squeeze that broke two ribs before I yanked myself through. I shake my head at my stupidity and go around. I can see the best way through tight squeezes with little effort now, but I was blind to them back then.

I'm a creature of the underworld, I think. So much so that I wonder if I could ever adjust to a normal life above ground again. Depression sweeps through me, but my thoughts of living in the outside world are not its source. I've reached the birthing ground of the feeders—what I call egg-monsters.

This is where Ninnis broke me. I was left, alone and terrified, with no food, water or weapons. And every three days, a man-eating egg-monster full of shark teeth would dangle down from the ceiling in a gelatinous womb before hatching, and trying to eat me. I found out later that the feeders were actually being birthed by Gaia, a breeder, whose enormously fat body was perched above a hole in the ceiling, far from view.

The place is just as I left it. And judging by the smell of dry blood and long since decomposed feeder bodies, the place hasn't been used for another breaking since.

Because I'm the last hunter, I remember. Ninnis told me that. After me, there won't be a need for human hunters anymore, because the Nephilim will no longer hide in the tight confines of the underworld. They will rule the overworld.

I step up to the ledge and look over the edge of the fifteen foot deep pit. Yellow crystals glow all around, like stars. I had such a hard time seeing in here during my breaking, but it seems bright to me now. I can see my bed of feeder skins against the far wall. The sight of it reminds me I'm exhausted. I leap the fifteen feet down and land with little effort. I had such a hard time climbing out of this pit. I could now make it out with three quick lunges, or just command the wind to lift me up.

But not now. Now it's time to sleep. I sit down on the bed of feeder skins and remember how to position myself on it for optimum comfort. After unclipping Whipsnap and placing the weapon between my body and the wall, I lie down. With my head on my hands, I open my eyes one last time and take in the sideways view of my former prison. There is no egg-monster here. There never will be again. Gaia is gone. Ninnis is not waiting outside the door. And after I sleep, I will finish my journey to the surface. I allow myself a brief smile, and then fall asleep.

When I awake, everything is different. I'm still looking at a sideways view of the feeder pit, but it smells different. The odors are…fresh.

"I knew you'd come here, Solomon."

My insides twist. It's Ninnis. I'm too frightened to reply.

"You always did make my job easy," he says. "Well, except for when you remembered who you were, but now that we're here, we can correct all that."

"I can leave whenever I want," I say, the words far more bold than I feel. But I have Whipsnap in my hands and am ready to defend myself. "You can't stop me."

"I won't need to," he says.

I hear a flicking sound. My memory says it's a lighter.

"You'll stay as long as it takes. Gaia will let me know when you're ready. Standard feeders won't break you this time, so she's prepared something special for you."

A hissing sound fills the chamber, but it's not organic. I

quickly climb the fifteen foot wall and look across the pit to the exit. Ninnis is gone. In his place is a bright flame shooting bits of orange like a Fourth of July sparkler. A wick.

He's going to collapse the tunnel!

I take two steps toward the feeder den's only exit when the dynamite explodes. The force of the blast slaps me backwards. I slam into the wall and then fall fifteen feet back into the pit. I'm unconscious before I hit the floor and don't feel the pain until I wake up again.

But the pain wracking every inch of my body holds my attention for only a moment. A wet slurping sound draws my eyes to the ceiling where a large wet sack slides out of the gloom and into view. Gaia is giving birth.

14

My heart rate hits hummingbird speeds as I watch the oozing, fleshy sack descend to the floor. I reach for Whipsnap, searching around with my hands, afraid to look away for even a moment. When I can't find my weapon, my panic skyrockets. I have no choice but to turn around. I see it lying five feet away among a pile of discarded feeder bones. A pile I accumulated during my stay here.

I dive for the weapon, snatch it up and spin around. Despite my belief that the feeder is already upon me, the thing has not yet hatched. The teardrop womb rests on the floor, still connected to Gaia far above by a pulsing umbilical.

This is the best time to strike. When the feeder is still trapped in the womb, defenseless and unaware of the danger. But I can't bring myself to attack. Not yet. I've faced feeders and killed them as myself—as Solomon—when I was first brought here, but it was in self-defense at first. And then for food. This would be neither, because I still have rations and can easily hide from the feeder at the top of the fifteen foot wall. My rations will eventually run out, but I don't want to kill something if I don't have to. Even if it is a Nephilim.

The birth sack stretches as the thing inside tries to break free. But the shape is all wrong. This is no feeder. It's something else. Something taller.

Fingers poke through the womb's skin. Human fingers. A second set of fingers pokes through and pulls. The two hands pull apart, sheering the womb away. Thick fluid oozes out onto the floor. The crouched creature stands up, cloaked in shadow, silhouetted by the wall of glowing crystals behind it. I can't yet make out the details, but the shape is decidedly human. A woman, I think. But her movements are stiff and awkward.

A thousand questions rush through my mind, but before I can attempt to answer even one of them, she catches my scent. So she has something in common with the feeders. They're ravenously hungry when born. Her head snaps in my direction. Though I can't yet see her eyes, I can feel them on me, sizing me up. She's more intelligent than the other feeders, who spent little time thinking before pouncing.

Perhaps I can reason with her? I think.

She hisses.

Probably not.

I raise Whipsnap in my hands, letting her see the spiked mace and sharp blade, hoping it will make her think twice. I have no intention of using the weapon—if she attacks I'll scale the wall and see if she follows—but *she* doesn't know that.

I'm startled when she leaps through the air, cutting the distance between us in half. She's fast, strong and will have no trouble following me out of the pit. Ninnis has thought of everything it seems. I'll have no choice but to fight, and kill, this person.

But it's not a person, I remind myself. As much as this thing looks human, it is Nephilim. And I still have no problem killing them. *This isn't enough to break me*, I think. *I can do this.*

She's only twenty feet from me now. Her body is covered in goopy red birth fluid, which is different from normal feeders. Her face is hidden behind a curtain of shoulder length black hair. It's been so long since I've seen anyone without a full head of blood red hair that my eyes linger on the hair. Something about it is familiar. The way it parts and descends in wet waves that will curl as they dry.

Oh God. Please, no.

My fear is confirmed when it speaks. "Solomon."

"No!" I scream. "Not her!"

"Solomon, come here."

I've heard her say that before. The voice is perfect. How is that possible?

It's not, I think. The only way she could be here, is if she was *really* here.

"Solomon," she says, bending to one knee and stretching her arms out toward me. "It's *so* good to see you, son."

Tears blur my eyes. "Mom?"

"Yes, Solomon. Come hug me."

I'm stuck in place, rooted like some ancient tree. Part of me wants to rush forward and wrap my arms around her. But I also remember how she moved a moment ago. My mother wasn't—isn't—that athletic. And the hiss. But her voice. It's her. It has to be.

I take a step forward, but stop again.

She called me "son." My mother never called me, "son." I have imagined reuniting with my parents several times. If my mother—my real mother—were to see me, she would rush up and hug me whether I was holding Whipsnap or not. She would trust me. She would weep loudly. I look up at the woman, arms still outstretched, waiting calmly for me to approach.

This is *not* my mother.

I flash back to a memory. I'm four. My mother is reading *Are You My Mother?* to me despite me being fully capable of reading it to her. Even before I could read, I had the story memorized and could recite it. But I liked the scary snort and the sound of my mother's voice when she read, "I know who you are. You are a bird, and you are my mother."

"You," I say, "Are not my mother."

She stands and brushes the hair from her face, tucking it behind her ears.

I step back with a gasp.

It *is* my mother. Her face. Her eyes. Her hair.

My mind reels for a moment, but I still know, without a doubt, that this thing birthed from the belly of Gaia is not who she claims to be. "You are *not* my mother!" I scream.

My faux-mother grins, revealing several rows of shark-like teeth.

Like I said, not my mother.

She leaps forward, hands reaching out for me, mouth stretched open. If it reaches me, this thing will tear me to shreds and eat every bit of flesh off my bones.

But it won't get close.

Its bold attack poses little threat.

And because it's a Nephilim, I feel no guilt turning Whipsnap's blade tip toward its chest.

She sees the blade coming and shouts, "No!" Her eyebrows turn up in fear.

And for a moment, I'm unsure.

But then the blade has struck, piercing ribcage and lung all at once. The perfect kill shot. Ull would be proud.

She staggers back, pulling the blade from her chest. Blood flows in chugs as her heart pumps it from her body. "Solomon," she says, "How could you?"

I want to tell her to shut up, that she's not my mother, but I can't speak. Because her face and voice are my mother's.

I step closer.

She backs away.

Her fear wounds me.

She falls to her knees. "I love you, Sol."

The words strangle me. I weep openly, watching her life ebb.

"My baby," she says. "At least I got to see you one...more...time."

She dies at my feet.

Now that she's no longer trying to kill me, she looks exactly like my mother. My dead mother. That I killed.

I drop to my knees beside her and lean my head against hers.

"I'm sorry, mom. I'm so sorry."

My face is wet with tears and snot and I remember the last time I felt guilt like this. It was when Ninnis first began stalking me. It was at night. And snowing. And when Aimee snuck up behind me, I thought she was him. One punch. I threw *one* punch and knocked her out cold. I was consumed by guilt afterwards. But it wasn't my fault.

It was Ninnis.

This was Ninnis.

Anger begins to replace my sadness as I realize Ninnis's plan. One by one, I'll be forced to kill my mother, my father, and who knows who else from my past until I no longer care.

I will kill them.

I will eventually eat them to survive.

And I…

Will…

Break.

I pull back from the body of this mother-shaped feeder. With my face turned to the ceiling, I fill my lungs and scream, "NINNIS!"

As my thunderous voice echoes in the pit, something else happens.

The solid stone floor beneath my feet—it shakes.

15

My fall is broken by my mother's—the feeder's—body. The earthquake knocked me from my feet. Several of the glowing yellow crystals in the walls popped free. Bones rattled. And high above, in the dark recess of the ceiling that is beyond my view, Gaia shrieks. It is the first time she has revealed her presence in this place.

The tremor was not part of Ninnis's plan.

But what was it?

My first inclination is to write it off as a normal earthquake. But nothing here is normal. It felt like the pounding foot falls of Behemoth, but I know there are no caverns large enough to hold that monster anywhere near here. Maybe it was caused by the explosion Ninnis set off? I shake my head. The earthquake didn't originate from that side of the cavern.

It originated…from me. The timing is the giveaway. At the height of my emotions, when I released my anger, the solid stone shook with my rage.

I never realized how complete my connection with Antarctica had become. I'd manipulated the air, mostly. Sometimes water. And snow. But I had never turned my attention fully to controlling stone. And here I am, believing myself entombed by the very earth to which I am bound, the earth that might well move when I command it.

I push myself away from my faux-mother, intent on escape. The three dimensional mental map I've created of the surrounding tunnels plays through my mind. Ninnis no doubt waits outside the destroyed entrance. Gaia lurks above. I turn my focus in the direction opposite of Ninnis, mentally working my way through the underground in search of a tunnel that will take me up, and away from this horrible place.

I find a tunnel leading slowly upward, where it connects to another tunnel, one I know very well. It is the tunnel Ninnis took me through when I was kidnapped. The very same tunnel where I once hid the Polaroid picture I now carry with me at all times. It will not only take me to the surface, it will take me to Clark Station Two, and my past.

The thought of facing that place again frightens me almost as much as facing whatever creature Gaia births next, but I can't stay here. I can't face even one more of those things.

The stone at the side of the pit is rough against my hand. I place my other hand against it, not knowing if physical touch is required, but it seems to make sense. I guess. I don't really know. But it feels right, so I close my eyes, push on the stone and will it to—

—what?

Open?

Disintegrate?

Compress?

Nothing happens, and I think it's because I really need to decide how this is going to work. It's not like moving air or water.

Or is it?

Everything is composed of atoms. Some are more loosely packed, like water or air, and others are tightly packed, like stone. Perhaps when I shift the wind, I'm really moving the atoms? But maybe the connection is even deeper than that? When people have strong emotions, it's reflected in their bodies. Extreme stress can destroy an immune system. Happy people are healthier and live longer. So do people with dogs. And unhappy people, well, they die faster and often on Monday mornings.

And when I have extreme emotions, the environment here reacts. The winds often reacts to my fear, occasionally saving me from a fall or projectile. Storms brew when I panic. And now, the earth itself shakes at my rage. It's as though this continent—a land as vast as the United States—is now part of my physical body. Perhaps that's why I don't feel temperature changes? I *am* the temperature. I can't feel it any more than I can the individual organs in my own body.

I don't control the environment. I don't manipulate this external thing. I am it. It is me.

But it is also beyond me. I'm used to controlling my small human body, not an entire continent. I don't think my brain, or any brain could handle that much sensory input. Thankfully, the continent seems to be on autopilot, much like the human heart or lungs—involuntary muscles that require no actual thinking.

Carving a hole through the earth is voluntary. Something I need to focus on to achieve.

So I take a deep breath, clear my mind and imagine the earth opening. I see myself stretching out into the stone, comingling atoms. The ground starts to shake. My heart races as I exert a kind of force I never have before. I slide my hands apart. A loud crack echoes in the chamber. The shaking grows more intense.

I scream as muscles in my arms burn. My head pounds with every heartbeat. And then, when I can't take any more, I fall to the ground gasping like I've just nearly drowned. My vision goes black for a moment, but three deep breaths clear my eyes and I see it. A tunnel, barely big enough to squeeze through has been opened in the stone wall.

But is it deep enough? Does it reach through two hundred feet of stone?

Too exhausted to stand, I drag myself toward the mouth of the tunnel and smell the air. It is dank and old. Like the pit. I have failed and lack the energy to try again. I'll have to face another feeder, and—

My hair twitches, tickling the side of my face. A breeze blows across my face, carrying the scents of snow and a hint of salt water. The smells of the surface!

Invigorated by the odor of freedom, I pull myself to my feet, but find my legs wobbly beneath my weight. Using Whipsnap as a cane, I hobble into the tunnel, and lean against the wall, scraping my shoulder with each step.

When I get ten feet into the tunnel, Gaia must sense I'm no longer in the pit because she starts shrieking. Ninnis will know I've escaped somehow, but it will take him time to clear the debris from the entrance. Then again, maybe he'll drop down from the ceiling where Gaia is hiding. I do my best to ignore the pain and exhaustion wracking my body, and focus on the remaining one hundred and ninety feet.

Each step feels like a knife in my stomach, and I'm fighting the urge to vomit, not because I need what little food is in there or because it would be gross, but because the scent would be easy to track. And I don't want Ninnis to know where I've gone.

I stumble out of my escape route and into the larger tunnel that leads to the surface. I've nearly reached my goal, but now must cover my tracks. If Ninnis finds and follows my new tunnel here, he'll know where I've gone. If he found me now, I would be in real danger. If he finds me after I close this tunnel, I would be defenseless.

I place my hands on the sides of the tunnel, close my eyes and grit my teeth. With the last of my energy, I bring my hands together and feel the stone closing. But not all of it. More than half the tunnel remains open, and Ninnis will follow it. But he will not find me. It will be as though I disappeared.

I slide to my knees. Sweat pours from my forehead. My body shivers. It will soon shut down.

After wrapping Whipsnap around my waist, I crawl on my hands and knees, following the tunnel up. The pain and physical trauma take me back to my past. I was eight. It was winter. I had dug a fort in the snow pile across the street from our house. My mother called me in for lunch and on my way back, I decided to pole vault a puddle with my shovel. Little did I know the sidewalk was sheer ice. When I landed, my feet shot out from under me and I fell flat on my back. The air exploded from my lungs and my whole back tensed with pain. Eight years old and I thought I was dying. I pulled myself, using just my arms, past two houses, and then up the stairs to my house, where I remained in bed for three days.

I'm repeating that memory now, crawling to safety while my body reels from a sudden and horrible punishment. While I know I'm not dying this time, I know I might if I linger. I reach the top of the tunnel fifteen minutes later and slide out onto the snow covered mountainside. Clark Station Two is just a mile away; most of the trip is downhill.

I can make it, I tell myself. *Just push harder.*

So I push.

I emerge from the tunnel and onto the snow like a new born seal. Gravity does the rest. The snow is packed tight and I slip over it, gaining speed with each passing second. I lie on my back, watching the clouds pass through the dark blue sky.

I see a bunny, I think, blinking my eyes at a rabbit shaped cloud. It's been so long since I've seen a bunny.

I blink again. My head lolls to the side. Cruising down the mountainside like a bobsled freed from the track, I blink one last time, seeing stones whizzing past.

And then I fall asleep.

16

I wake to a world of glowing white light. It wraps around me, holding me tight. I can't move my head. Or my limbs. But I can feel my eyes shifting, so I know I'm actually seeing the white light. It's not in my head. I flex my arms with a grunt, but am still stuck. The sound of my voice is muffled. Contained.

I'm trapped, I think, and I fight my bonds with all my strength. A crack forms in the white. It's close to my eyes, so I have to strain to focus on it. When I do, the reality of my current predicament slams home.

I'm not only trapped, I'm frozen—in ice!

My heart races. Each breath comes faster than the last.

I can breathe, I realize.

Maybe some parts of me are still free of the ice. If only I could feel cold, I would know! Of course, if I could feel cold, I would be dead.

With the realization that I won't die any time soon, I begin to calm and think about my situation in a more rational way. I fell asleep while sliding down the mountainside. And I somehow ended up buried by snow—an avalanche maybe—which melted around my warm body and then refroze while I slept.

But more comforting than that is the knowledge that this ice, no matter how much of it is surrounding me, is part of the Antarctican environment, and as such, part of me. I focus on the ice and try a new trick. I can't feel temperature variations, but I still might be able to warm things up a few degrees. I picture the water molecules, bound tightly together. *Move*, I will them, *vibrate!* When a drop of water strikes my eye, causing me to blink, I know it's working.

The white light grows brighter. Then becomes tinged with blue. And then—daylight.

"Argh!" I scream, as I look directly into the sun.

The remaining ice and snow surrounding my body explodes away from me as I sit up and cup my hands over my eyes. Two bright green and purple circles dance in my vision. When the pain subsides, I fumble blindly through my belongings and dig out the sunglasses Ninnis gave me—gave Ull—to use on the surface. I haven't had to use for them in ages, but they are essential for visiting the outside during the day time. I'm like a vampire now, unable to bear the daylight. And it's not just my eyes. My skin is so fair now that I'll burn quickly without clothing.

Even with the sunglasses on, I have to squint so hard that my vision is almost nothing. So I almost miss the structure behind me when I look around. But the ribbed surface of the steel catches my attention. The top of a rounded structure is poking out of the snow.

Most of the surface is covered in snow, but I can see bits of gray. I climb atop it, crawling over its bumpy surface, feeling the metal with my hands. It's a roof. The roof of Clark Station Two! My excitement mixed with my near blindness hides a ridge in the hard surface and when I shift forward again, the metal beneath my hands falls away.

I plummet forward and am swallowed whole by the buried structure. My landing is pitiful, like I'm a nerdy little kid tripping over his shoelaces again. But I'm not upset. I'm laughing, because when I open my eyes, I recognize where I am.

"Clark Station Two," I say to myself. "I'm back."

The place does not return my greeting. Some of the place has been rearranged; the couch is in a different spot. And some of the equipment is missing—like the computer. But the space remains the same. I sit up and find that I'm lying in the very spot where Aimee lay unconscious after I slugged her. That was just moments before I ventured out into the night on a mission to restart the generator. A mission that ended with my abduction.

Back on my feet, I dust the snow and debris from my body and head for what was—for a day—my room. The hallway running straight down the center of the hanger-like building has doors on either side. Mine is the third on the left.

When I open it, a bell rings further down the hallway. The sound strikes me like a baseball bat to the gut. The bell. It rang the night I left this room, alerting Dr. Clark and Aimee that I was awake. It's what sent her after me. I shake my head, wishing for a moment that I did not have a photographic memory. The past sometimes replays itself when I least expect it.

Of course, sometimes the past doesn't even need to be re-played to have an effect on me. I open the door and find my suitcase on the floor between the small desk and unmade cot. They left it here. They left everything I brought with me. *They really thought they would find me*, I think. I fall to my knees, unzip the luggage and stare down at my clothes. I sit there, hands shak-ing, and pick up a black turtleneck. I bring it to my face, and breathe in.

I've read that scent is the biggest trigger for memories. As the smell of my mother's favorite fabric softener tickles my nose, I know it's true. My body tenses as I squeeze the fabric against my face and let out a desperate wail. This was the smell of my child-hood. Of my innocence. I wore it, like a cologne, every day of my life before being taken from this place.

When I start to hyperventilate I realize that revisiting the past like this might be just as bad for me as facing down replicas of my parents in the pit. It's breaking me.

No, I think, *it's remaking me*. This is a good pain. I can find strength here.

For the moment. If Ninnis knew I would return to the pit, he'll eventually come looking here. Apparently my sentimentality is predictable, and a weakness. But what about Clark Station One? Does Ninnis know about that location? Has he ever visited the place of my birth? It was buried by snow fairly fast. It's worth the risk, I think. From the moment I first set foot on Antarctica, I have felt drawn to Clark Station One. Perhaps I will find the strength I need to face the Nephilim there?

I wipe away my tears and try to pull the dark turtleneck over my head. It doesn't fit. Not even close. I hold the shirt up in front of me and wonder if it somehow shrunk. But then I remember what I looked like in it. Skinny and frail. I look at my arm next to the sleeve. Muscles twitch beneath my pale skin. I've gotten bigger.

A lot bigger.

None of these clothes will fit me, which is probably a good thing because aside from the turtleneck, the bright 1980's wardrobe will stand out like a beacon on the snow. I tear a chunk of fabric from the shirt and stuff it in the pouch with the photo.

"What I need," I say, longing to hear a voice in this place, "is something white."

I check the room next to mine. It's empty, but I can tell it belonged to my parents. Their scent lingers. I close the door quickly, not wanting to repeat my emotional episode. The next two rooms I check are empty. The fourth smells like Old Spice. Dr. Clark's room.

Which would make the room next door… I pause, hand on the knob. If this room is anything but empty, I'm going to have a hard time, and even without Ull present, I'm kind of getting sick of crying. But I can't not go in. So I pretend I'm facing down a feeder and simply act. I twist the doorknob and step in.

Nothing on the cot. The freestanding closet is open, and empty. The floor is clear. And the desk…the desk holds an envelope.

With my name on it.

I wonder for a moment if I've been trapped. Did Ninnis

know I would come here? Did he leave this for me? Is he outside right now? I step back from the envelope, but the idea of leaving it feels unbearable. I step forward and look at my name written on it. It's just three letters—SOL—but the writing is familiar. I take out the Polaroid photo and look at the hand writing: Mira and Sol…

The handwriting is the same. Mira wrote this.

For me.

I take the envelope in a shaking hand and find the old glue easy to pull away. Inside is a single lined piece of paper, dated the day before Ninnis took me. I read the note:

Solomon,

I am new to this and I'm not good at writing so I'm going to get right to the point. I like you. A lot. I'm not big on romance. Or flowers. Or girly things in general. So if that is okay with you, I'll overlook the fact that you are clumsy. And smart. And kind. We will always be good friends. I knew it from the moment I picked you up off of my driveway. But maybe, if you're lucky, we can be something more? I'm debating about whether or not to give this to you, because the idea of you turning me down makes me sick to my stomach. Actually, I'm pretty sure that this will make you sick to your stomach, too. So to make this simple I'm going to do something I swore I would never do.

Do you like me? □ Yes. □ No.

Or maybe just sit next to me and put your foot against mine. Grin.

Mira.

I read the letter twice more before returning it to the envelope and placing it back on the desk. I cannot describe how it makes me feel, because I'm feeling too many emotions at the same time. Mira, who was the first and only girl to give me the time of day, never mind her heart, had planned to give this to me the day I disappeared.

I back out of the room and close the door. It's a memento of my past too painful to take with me, because it doesn't just remind me of my past—of what I once had—it represents the life I *could* have had. The happiness. The love. It's more than I can bear.

The door behind me swings open when I bump into it. I turn and find a room full of gear and clothing. For a moment I worry that someone's been living here, but then I smell oil and see the toolbox. This was Collette's room. She was a loud, rude, joke-telling mechanic. She must have jumped ship and left everything behind.

Piles of clothes fall out of the closet when I tug on the handle. But a lone, white winter snowsuit remains hung.

"Thank you, Collette," I say.

Collette was a big woman—at least she seemed that way back then—so the suit is a little loose on me, but just barely. My mom would say I'll grow into it. I find a pair of white winter boots, wrap a white t-shirt around my lower face and pull the hood up over my red hair. Standing on the white surface of Antarcica, only my sunglasses will show, and if I need to be invisible, I can take them off.

The new gear lifts my spirits. I will be hard to find now as the surface winds carry away my scent and the snowsuit keeps me invisible. I turn to leave, but spot a pen on the desk. I pick it up, click it a few times, and smile.

I return to Mira's room and open the note.

I check off, "☐ Yes."

17

After collecting a few more items, a Zippo lighter, some white gloves, a whetstone and—ahem—a comb, I stand beneath the hole in the ceiling and look up. The blue sky greets me. Its brightness makes me feel alive, despite the pain it causes my sunglasses covered eyes. I'm wearing the white snowsuit and boots. A tiny sliver of my forehead is my only exposed skin. Otherwise I look like some kind of modern abominable snowman. Well, except for the fact that I'm wearing my belt, and Whipsnap, on top of the suit. If I need additional stealth, I can fit them inside the suit.

The exit is twenty feet above me. I didn't get a good look at it before, but I can see now that the hole was punched in from above. I'm not the first person here. Which means I *really* need to go.

I leap up, hands outstretched and create a burst of wind that carries me up, but isn't nearly enough to exhaust me. I grasp the edge of the hole with my gloved hands and slip a little. But I dig down tight and hoist myself up. Eighth grade gym class enters my mind. I had already skipped a few grades, but my ten-year-old age didn't deter Mrs. Edelstein. I was in eighth grade so they would test my physical prowess against the other eighth grade boys. Joey Dimarco did thirty chin ups. I couldn't manage one. Even Mrs Edelstein couldn't hold back a laugh. How things have changed.

I yank myself up with little effort, bounding from the hole and landing on the metal roof. "Eat your heart out, Joey Dimarco."

I stare out at the view before me. A sliver of ocean cuts across the horizon. I consider heading to the water. Food would be plentiful. Lots of places to hide, especially since I could swim in the ocean and not freeze. But I think about the killer whales and leopard seals. I don't think either species are traditionally man-eaters, but you never know when one will decide to try something new. Then again, maybe—

The wind shifts.

I smell someone behind me.

Someone new.

I spin around while silently cursing myself for not scanning the area before coming out of the hole. Just because I'm not underground doesn't mean I shouldn't live by the same rules!

The mountains behind me come into view. The man standing in front of them is so well camouflaged in white that I almost looked right past him. When I do see him, there isn't even a single moment I consider whether this is friend or foe, because he's got an arrow nocked in a bow, pointed directly at my head. Even still, I might normally try to talk someone out of this situation, but he's already released his grip and sent the arrow flying toward my head.

Before I can even think it, a strong burst of wind shoots up and knocks the arrow off course. I've faced this challenge before when I fought Ull and his giant arrows. My body—including the whole of Antarctica—is reacting on instinct.

Snow bursts up between me and the hunter, concealing my actions for a moment. But I don't move. Ull would have pressed the attack, taken advantage of the snowy distraction. He's a predator. I prefer to think before I act, and sometimes that includes speaking. I know his arrows can't reach me, so I take Xin's advice and try to make friends.

"You don't have to fight," I say.

A second arrow shoots my way and passes over my head.

I never was good at making friends.

The man, like me, is covered in white fabric from head to toe. But he's not wearing sunglasses. His eyes blaze blue between the hood and mask covering his lower face. The sun doesn't bother him at all. *How long has he been topside?*

A third arrow is quickly nocked and fired, but I notice he's no longer aiming at my face. He's aiming at my knees! In a flash I realize he's compensating for the vertical wind pushing his arrows above me. The second shot was much closer than the first, and this one might actually strike me!

The bow *twangs* loudly as he lets the arrow fly.

I shift to my right and throw my hands to the left, physically directing which way the wind should blow. The arrow is just inches from my face when the horizontal wind strikes it. I feel a tug on my hood as it passes.

Now the hunter is confused, circling me slowly.

I stand my ground and say, "What is your name?"

"You know my name," he replies, his voice tinged with a German accent.

"Actually," I say, raising an index finger like some college professor postulating a point.

Crunch, crunch, crunch.

Someone is running through the snow behind me. The hunter has not come alone!

I grasp Whipsnap and pull. The weapon snaps open in my hand and I turn to face my attacker.

"Em, wait!" the man shouts.

Normally I'd tune out anything someone shouted while I'm about to be pounced upon, but the shortened name—Em—fills my mind as I catch site of the second hunter. It's a girl. Like the man, she's clothed in all white, but she's a good foot shorter than me and has wide hips. Well, not wide for a girl, but wide for a boy. A glint of sunlight on metal brings my eyes to her hands, where she holds two daggers, one of which is now swiping toward my midsection.

Like Kainda, it would be a mistake for me to underestimate this hunter simply because she's a girl. In fact, as someone who spent most of his life being out-muscled by the opposite sex, this should be second nature to me by now. I leap back, bending my stomach out of the way. The blade flashes past my stomach, scratching the fabric of my snowsuit.

Crunch, crunch, crunch.

The man is approaching now, too. He sounded worried

about the girl and probably gave up on the arrows because his erratic shooting might strike her.

The girl strikes again. I block the blow with Whipsnap, bend the weapon back and let it spring out as I spin to face the man. The girl shouts in surprise as Whipsnap sweeps out her legs and knocks her onto her back.

"Em!" the man shouts again, uncommonly worried for a hunter.

For a moment I wonder if this man is a hunter at all, but then I see the blades attached to the top and bottom of his bow, which he now holds like a staff, and I know without a doubt that this weapon was dreamed up in the nightmare of the underworld.

Whipsnap collides with the bladed bow again and again as the man attacks and I parry. Each of his strikes is aimed to kill, and several come close. If this does not end soon, I will surely die.

The man thrusts. The blade passes by my face, missing by inches.

I have him now. His stomach is open. Whipsnap's blade is pointed at his gut. All I need to do is thrust.

But I don't.

I can't.

Instead, I apply hundreds of pages of ninja magazine fighting technique tutorials stored in my perfect memory. I take hold of his jacket with my left hand and leap. I place my feet against his stomach and let his momentum and my weight pull us to the ground. When we strike, I thrust with my legs and send the man flying. For good measure, I add a gust of wind to take him five feet further. The impact should give him something to think about.

But as the man sails through the air, he shouts, "Epsilon! Like we practiced!"

Epsilon?

I hear the girl shifting as she stands. Her face is masked, but I can sense a grin there.

The man lands like a cat, rolling back to his feet, an arrow already being nocked.

The girl opens her jacket, revealing a belt and two crisscrossing straps over her chest, which are absolutely laden with throwing blades. She lets the first one fly just as the man fires an arrow. As the wind kicks up around me I realize that Epsilon is code for some kind of practiced attack. The arrows and knives will come like hail from a storm and I'm not sure I can deflect them all without also compromising my body. Either way, these two have the upper hand.

I need Ull, but there is no time to free him. The first knife flips past my head, causing me to duck directly into the path of an incoming arrow.

18

If not for the wind acting as my instinctive guardian, I would be dead. The arrow coming for my head bends as the wind carries it up and just over my nose. But there is no time to think about how lucky I am, because two more knives and another arrow are coming my way.

A combination of quick movements and wind gusts keep the blades from striking their target, but each shot comes closer than the last. I will the wind to carry snow and obscure my attacker's view, but I'm moving fast, and the gusts must continually change directions; only a few flakes shift on the ground.

"Aim wide!" the man shouts. "I'll force him to you."

At first I think they've made a mistake, announcing their intentions, but I quickly realize it doesn't matter. She's now throwing where I'm not, while he's aiming where I am. No matter where I go, a blade awaits me.

I twist and spin Whipsnap in front of me. A knife blade is deflected, and an arrow dodged, but the hunters are running around me now, throwing and shooting from so many different directions that they're impossible to keep track of.

Epsilon is a genius attack, I think, before the first blade—a knife—strikes my left arm. The sharp dagger slices through my coat and the top few layers of my skin. It's a superficial wound, but I'm sure it's the first of many.

"Stop!" I shout. "You don't need to kill me!"

"Don't listen to him, Em!" the man shouts.

"It's us or him!"

"I don't want to kill you," I say with a grunt as an arrow forces me to twist around. A knife handle strikes my leg. For a moment I think I've been stabbed and take my eyes off of the hunters to look at the wound. I realize the distraction will probably cost me my life, but it doesn't. Instead, the subtle downward shift of my head saves my life.

The arrow headed for my right eye grazes my forehead and pierces my hood instead, yanking it off my head.

But the sudden shift of my hood has removed my sunglasses as well. The bright sky and sun glaring off the snow blinds me. My eyes clench shut. I'm blind.

The girl shouts, "Father wait!" A knife flies toward me. I can hear it whipping through the air.

Father? Since when do father and daughter hunters work together?

I hear the twang of an arrow being shot.

The weapons will reach me simultaneously.

There is a loud crack in front of my face. I flinch away from it, wondering if I've been hit, but I haven't yet felt the pain.

"Em, *why?*" the father says. I can hear him nocking another arrow, but he does not fire. "You cannot hesitate with their kind."

"But that's the problem," she says, her voice devoid of the man's German accent. I can hear her walking toward me. "He's not *their* kind." She stops next to me and whispers, "If you move I will bury my blade in your throat." She takes hold of my hair and lifts it up. "He's *our* kind."

The man hustles toward me. "Don't move. I'm too close to miss."

"I'm not moving," I say.

He stops above me. I can feel him looking at me. At my hair, but why?

"Show me your face," he says.

I look up and try to open my eyes, but the brightness is unbearable.

"I do not recognize him, father," Em says.

"What is your name?" the man asks.

"Solomon. Solomon Vincent."

"What are you doing here?"

"I was taken from here." I point to the buried roof of Clark Station Two. "I stayed there. With my parents."

"What kind of parents would bring a child here?" the man asks rhetorically. "When did this happen?"

"Time is different in the underground," I say.

"The year," he says.

"Nineteen eighty-eight." Having answered, I can't help but wonder, "How long has it been?"

"I'm asking the questions," he says. "And if I do not like your answers, I *will* kill you."

"Father..." Em says.

"Quiet, Em," he replies. "We did not survive this long by entertaining guests."

His attention shifts back to me. "Who took you? Who broke you?"

"Ninnis," I say.

I hear the girl give a faint gasp.

"And your breeder? In the pit?"

"Gaia."

Another gasp.

I feel the tip of the man's arrow tickling my hair.

"And your master?"

I feel like the answer will be my death sentence, but giving another name might be just as bad. "Ull."

"No..." The girl whispers.

"You speak lies," the man says. "Ull would not lose another hunter. Certainly not one broken by Ninnis. It's not possible."

A single word repeats in my mind. *Another.* A puzzle begins to unravel in my mind. The man's voice sounds old, but not quite as old as Ninnis. His daughter is young, but here that means little, especially because of the way the underworld modifies time. And he's German. My mind flashes through pages of history books. Not a lot of people have come to Antarctica, and the majority of them have come in the past twenty years. In 1939, before World War Two, the Nazi's sent a large expedition to Antarctica. Some speculate that they were looking for evidence of an ancient civilization. Atlantis even. Some think they built a secret base where many Nazis escaped after the war. No one really knows what they did, but several men were reported missing. I flash through their names and ages and pick the most likely candidate.

"Anything is possible, *Tobias*."

He takes a step back, surprise disarming him for a moment.

"No one here knows my name," he says.

"You came to Antarctica in nineteen thirty-nine with the Nazis. You were a pilot. Your plane crashed while mapping the interior. The two men serving with you were later discovered, dead. But your body was never found. Because you had been taken. And broken. And you became a hunter." Images of Tobias handling the bow shift through my mind like a slideshow.

Another.

"Ull was *your* master, too. But you remembered yourself. You escaped with your daughter. And now you live on the surface, hiding from the hunters."

I can hear nothing but the wind for a moment. Then a sound like a growl rises up, and he kicks me in the gut. "Breeder abomination!"

I roll to the side. The hood falls back over my head, bringing my sunglasses forward again. As I struggle to my hands and knees, I pull the sunglasses back over my eyes. I turn toward the man and see the unbridled rage in his eyes. He's about to let that arrow blast through my head.

"Look at me," I say. "I'm human. I'm not like Xin."

Xin's name makes the man sneer. I'm digging my own grave here. Luckily, Em comes to my rescue.

"But father, his hair."

My hair…. My hair! The blond streak!

I sit upright. The arrow follows my head, but I'm not seeing it anymore. "Do you have it too?" I ask. "Is the red fading?"

My excitement disarms the man slightly. He lowers the arrow to my chest and looks back at Em as she removes her hood.

She's pretty, but skinny. Her blue eyes blaze like her father's. But it's her hair that holds my attention. Much of it is deep red, like mine, but at least a quarter of it is light brown.

Innocence regained. Like me.

I turn to the man. "And you?"

"Less than her," he says, and then raises his aim back to my head. "But more than *you*. How did you know those things about me?"

"I have a photographic memory," I say.

"This does not explain how you knew my name."

"It does," I assure him. "I…I read a lot before coming here. Science. Literature. History. In the outside world, your mission to Antactica is now part of the history of Germany leading up to World War Two."

His eyes widen. "A second world war? The Führer?"

"Invaded Poland. Then just about everywhere else in Europe."

"How many this time?"

"Dead?"

He nods.

"The highest number I read was seventy-eight—"

"Thousand?" he says.

"Million."

The arrow lowers as the number saps his desire to kill me.

"What are you talking about father?" Em asks.

"Do not tell her," he says to me. "It will taint her innocence."

His concern is noble, so I agree with a nod and get back to answering his original question. "I read about your expedition. There was mention of the plane crash. The names of the men on board. And the one that went missing."

"Several other men went missing on that expedition," he says.

"All here?" I ask.

He shakes his head. "Just one other. The rest were claimed by the land."

"I guessed at your name," I say. "You look like a Tobias."

He looks down at himself, hidden beneath layers of fabric. "You cannot see me."

"Okay," I say with a grin, "You *sound* like a Tobias."

Em lets out a snort.

"And Ull? How did you know that he was my master?"

I point to the bow.

"Ahh," he says.

"Plus you kind of smell like him."

Em laughs loudly now and despite clearly fighting it, Tobias smiles. The sight of his grin relaxes me and I allow myself a chuckle.

"It still doesn't make sense," he says. "That someone broken by Ninnis and subservient to Ull could manage to not only fight the mental bondage, but then also escape to the surface... You're fast, I'll grant you that. I've never seen someone dodge arrows like that. But escape, on your own, should have been impossible."

"You did it."

"We had help."

A surge of hope fills me. Not only have I met two free hunters, but they also escaped with help! There might be others.

"So how did you do it?" he asks again, his smile gone. "How did you escape from Ull?"

My grin fades, too, as the memory returns.

"It was easy," I say. "I killed him." I look Tobias in the eyes and add, "I took his own arrow and buried it in his forehead."

"Ull…is dead?"

"And buried," I say. "At New Jericho."

That last bit of information seems to confirm my story. Tobias suddenly roars with laughter. He falls to the snow, jubilant. Em and I watch him, half grinning, half concerned. Has the man gone mad? "I'm free," he says as his hood falls from his head and frees his shoulder length, red hair.

He shouts again, this time raising a victorious fist into the air, "I'm free!" And as his daughter embraces him, joining in his laughter, I see something amazing. A shock of the man's blood red hair turns brown.

Innocence reclaimed. I laugh with them.

19

I barely notice the five mile walk as I'm led to Tobias's and Em's hideout. We move in silence, vigilant against hunters—who might be looking for me, or for them. Despite the silence, my mind is alive with excitement. I have made friends. Allies. Skilled allies.

Of course, they don't yet know who I am. Who I really am. And the evil that lives inside me. But I will tell them soon. They need to know that I'm not just an average escapee. Not telling them would put them in more danger than I care to consider. If I'm to shed any more of this blood red hair—like Tobias—I must embrace everything the Nephilim abhor. I've done a good job with forgiveness, mercy and love, but need to add honesty to the mix.

I'm so lost in my thoughts that I fail to notice the shifting view of the mountains to my left. I just keep my eyes on the ground, following Tobias. We're walking along an old path, worn down by the occasional passage of modern man. The firm ice and treaded gouges left by numerous Sno-Cats ensure that we won't leave any footprints behind. My eyes linger on the tread marks. There have been fifteen thousand, five hundred and twenty-one grooves. I didn't mean to count them. I barely noticed I had. But when the number pops into my conscious thoughts, it snaps me from my reverie.

A sudden weakness sweeps through my body. I let out a grunt and fall to my knees.

Tobias is by my side in a flash. "Are you all right?"

I feel winded. Emotional. Desperately close to something. Something I have craved since I left Antarctica as a baby.

I've felt this intense draw once before. I look up and see the Sno-Cat tracks stretching toward the horizon.

"Is he okay?" Em asks.

I feel Tobias's hand on my shoulder. "I don't know," he says.

"We're there," I say.

His hand pulls away.

"How...did you know?"

"This is home," I say, looking to my left. Except for a shift in the white, snow-coated areas of the massive stone mountains, the view matches my memory perfectly.

"Solomon," Em says. "This *is* our home, but how did *you* know?"

"I've been here before."

Em turns to Tobias. "Is he the boy?"

"You dug in the ice," Tobias says. "Until you bled. We watched from a distance. I had to recover the small portion of ceiling you uncovered."

I nod briefly and take several deep breaths to steady myself. The emotional surge that caught me off guard is fading. *I need to get harder*, I think. If something like this happened at a crucial moment, I'd be dead. But how can I repel all things Nephilim while simultaneously becoming some kind of hard-hearted warrior? Isn't that exactly what they are?

"Solomon." Tobias's voice sounds serious. He senses I'm holding something back and it has him on edge. "When you dug in the ice. That wasn't your first time here, was it?"

With a shake of my head, I say, "No."

"Father," Em says. "I don't understand. This place has been buried for—" She gasps as something occurs to her.

She does that a lot, I think. *Gasping*. It's kind of a funny habit for a hunter—an ex-hunter.

"You don't think…" She crouches down in front of me, looking at my face, which is hidden behind a hood and sunglasses. "Are you him? Are you the baby?"

A thousand memories of this place, seen through the eyes of a baby, flash through my mind. Many of the memories involve the rusty ceiling as I lay on my back, but there are also smiling faces and cooing voices. My mother and father. Dr. Clark. Aimee. The emotions surge again, but I fight against them this time. If they start to see me as a blubbering, over-emotional nutcase, they might not trust me. And if they don't trust me, they will never help me. *I need allies*, I remind myself. *Pull it together*.

At least they can't see my face, so the effort I put into calming my voice and regaining my feet is hidden from them. "Yes," I say. "I was born here. This…was my home."

"It's *him*," Em says to her father, her voice a whisper. She digs into her coat, opening a pouch hidden within. She pulls out a small, white square. "It's you."

I take the paper from her hand and turn it over. It's a photo of a baby. A boy, I think. The photo is a Polaroid, like the one I carry around. The baby has bright blue eyes, a one inch ring of fuzz around its head and a goofy smile. The rainbow-striped, afghan blanket the baby lays on catches my attention. I've had it since they day I was born. My mother made it. "This photo is of *me*."

Tobias and Em look at each other. "Father, it's *him!*"

He turns to me and says, "It's a good thing we didn't kill you."

"Why, exactly, is that good thing?" I ask. I can think of several good reasons, but I'm a stranger to these people. Sure, they've been living in Clark Station One, and happened to find a photo of me, which is surprising, but I sense there is more going on here.

"You are the first and only son of Antarctica," Em says.

"Stories of your birth have been told in the underworld for years," Tobias says. "The Nephilim have been awaiting your return. *We* have been awaiting your return as well. I should have realized it was you that day, digging through the ice. How else could you have known about this place? I could have taken you then. Spared you the—"

I take a step back, my defenses coming up. "Taken me? You would have taken me, too? Are you no better than them?" I stab my finger downward.

"Solomon," he says, a little bit of sadness creeping into his voice. "Had I found you first, you would have been spared the breaking. The three tests. I could have trained you myself. The corruption would have never turned your hair red."

"But why take me at all?" I ask. "Why not protect me. Send me home? Warn the others?"

"Because," Em says. "We need you here. It is a fate that could not be avoided."

"I've known that since the day of your birth," Tobias says.

"How?" I ask.

Tobias pulls his mask down so I can see his face. "Because I witnessed it. I saw the light. The power of your birth shattered the ice and buried this place beneath thirty feet of snow." He steps closer. "Solomon, please trust that we mean you no harm. You are here now, and that is what is important."

While I do not like the fact that this man would have kidnapped me if given the chance, I do believe his motivation isn't necessarily evil. And life with Tobias would have been better than my life underground, with Ninnis. I would still retain my innocence. Nephil would not reside within me. And Aimee would not have been taken captive.

Tobias reaches out a welcoming hand toward me. "Come. See your home again. There is someone who would very much like to meet you."

"Who?" I ask.

"Luca. My son." He flashes a grin. "You two have a lot in common. Come, follow me."

He leads me to the entrance to Clark Station One, a tunnel

some two hundred feet away from the building. The entrance is cleverly disguised by a snow covered hatch. The first fifty feet of the downward sloping tunnel is so small that we have to slide down on our bellies. After that, it levels out and is tall enough to stand in.

"A defensive bottleneck?" I ask. Any enemy foolish enough to enter the tunnel could be easily dispatched before their whole body exited the small hole.

"Yes, yes," Tobias says with a dismissive wave of his hand. Then he's walking quickly toward the gray outer door of Clark Station One, which I can see ahead.

"I can't believe we didn't recognize you right away," Em says.

"From the baby photo?" I ask. "I've changed a lot since then."

"Mm," she says.

I absolutely hate it when someone rubs in the fact that they know something I don't, especially when it relates to me. Always have. It makes me feel stupid. And angry. So I change the subject. "Is Em short for something?"

"Emilie," she says. "With an I and an E at the end. Not a Y."

"The German spelling," I say.

She nods, and doesn't seem all that interested in my questions. Her eyes, like her father's, are glued to the door ahead of us.

"You don't have his accent," I say.

"An American teacher taught me how to speak English. I didn't see my father much when I was young. I didn't see him much at all, actually. Not until we escaped."

"How *did* you escape?" I ask.

"Not now," she says. "We're here."

We stop in front of the door. Tobias knocks two times, pauses and then knocks three times. The door opens from the inside and Tobias rushes inside. He bends over and scoops up a small body. "Solomon," he says, turning toward me. "I'd like you to meet my son, Luca."

I see the boy's eyes and my heart skips a beat. They look so familiar. When I look at the rest of his face, I immediately know why I know his eyes.

It's because they're mine.

Luca is *me*.

As a child.

"Luca," Tobias says. "This is Solomon—"

"—your brother."

20

The next hour is surreal as I give myself a tour of the place I where was born. But he's not me. Not really. Even though he is identical to me at six years old.

Identical.

Even his pure blond, unbroken hair. But he does not share my memories, and only some of my personality. I bring none of this up, because he is beyond excited to meet me and is leading me around by the hand, pointing out Tobias's room (my parents' room), Em's room (the Clarks' room) and his bedroom (my bedroom). He even sleeps in the makeshift crib—a cot with slabs of wood nailed around the sides to keep me from rolling out— that my father and Dr. Clark made for me. I look at its metal and wooden frame, now sporting a mattress of feeder skins, and look up. There is more rust on the ceiling than I remember, but it is still the same place.

I feel instantly at home and the smile on my face is genuine.

But I cannot stop thinking about the little me holding my

hand. How is he possible? Why is he here? Is he really my brother?

I feel sick to my stomach with the thought I maybe I had a twin who was taken at birth and maybe he's only six because he lived underground all this time?

The questions don't stop coming, so when the tour finishes in the living room I think I might get a chance to speak to Tobias in private. But Luca has other plans. He props himself up on my—his—bed. His little legs dangle over the side.

"Will I look like you when I'm older?" he asks.

The answer to that question is simple. Yes. You'll look exactly like me when you're older, but I don't think he knows the truth. He can see that we look alike, but he doesn't recognize his older face the way I do my younger. So I stick to the story. "Brothers often do. Some even look like twins."

"I wish we were twins," he says with a grin.

The kid has just met me, but I can see in his eyes that he's already idolizing me. It makes me uncomfortable and I can't help but wonder how much he's been told about me. And how much of it is true. "Why?" I ask.

"Because you're so big."

That's the first time in my life someone has called me big, and I almost argue, but let it go because most teenagers are big in comparison to a six year old boy. "That's it?"

He thinks for a moment and then his eyes go wide. He jumps down from the bed and fishes out a cardboard box from underneath it. Inside are several drawings on water damaged sheets of paper and five very worn crayons. I wonder what will happen when he runs out of crayons? Or paper. It will be a sad day for him.

He shoves a piece of paper in my face. On it is a small boy. And a very tall man. Both look angry. It's hard to tell what they're doing, but Luca translates it for me.

"It's you," he says. "You're fighting the bad men."

"Bad men?"

"I'm not allowed to say their names."

"How did you know I would fight the bad men?"

"Father told me." Luca flips to the next drawing.

The giant is on the ground. I think he's dead. And the boy stands above him. *On top of him.* That's when I see the large arrow sticking out of the giant's head. I take the picture and sit down in an old metal folding chair next to the room's desk.

"I saw you," Luca whispers. He pulls the drawing down so we're looking eye to eye. "I saw you do it."

It seems impossible—only Ninnis saw what really happened the day I killed Ull. No one else knows. Is Luca some kind of a prophet? "What else do you see?"

"Just the big things. When they happen. Like dreams."

"You can't see what's going to happen?"

He shakes his head, no.

"Can you see anyone else?"

No again. "Just you."

Footsteps approach. "Don't tell father," he says, snatching away the drawing and putting it back in the box. "He doesn't know."

Em arrives in the doorway, but Luca is still nervous. He puts his hands behind his back and tries to hide his smile by pushing out his lower lip with his tongue. I used to do the same thing. It's a dead giveaway that mischief is afoot.

Em squints at him. She's got thin eyes already and they essentially disappear. Her face is wide, but pretty, and her cheeks are covered in freckles. At least half of her straight hair is brown. She's also not nearly as pale as me. *They've been on the surface for some time,* I think.

"What are you two up to?" she asks.

Luca's smile can't be contained. He's guilty of something, but says nothing.

"Brother stuff," I say.

"Yeah," says Luca. "Brother stuff."

"Not sister stuff?" Em says.

Luca sticks out his tongue.

Em tugs on my shirt. After meeting Luca, Tobias gave me a pair of old jeans and a flannel shirt that I think belonged to Dr. Clark. I never saw him in it, but I've seen him in many others like it. The clothes are too big for me, but I look almost normal for the first time in years.

Years...

"Father wants to speak to you now," she says, motioning with her head for me to follow.

Luca starts to follow us, but Em stops him. "Just Sol."

"Aww," Luca says with a stomp of his foot, but he turns around and goes back into his room.

Em looks back at me and sees my funny grin. "What?"

"Nothing."

She stops. "*What?*"

"You called me Sol. Reminds me of home. Of my family. It's…it's nice."

"Oh," she says. "Good."

She leads me to my parents' old room, now Tobias's and stops by the door. "You can think of us like that now if you want. Like family. Did you have a sister before?"

"I was an only child," I tell her.

"Sad."

"I had a friend. Justin. He was like family. Like a brother."

"Well," she says. "Now you have a sister. And a little brother."

I smile wide. "Thanks."

She opens the door for me and stands aside. Tobias stands with his back to me.

"Come in, Solomon," he says. "Close the door behind you."

I do.

"I want to tell you everything, Solomon. About me. About Emilie. And about Luca."

I see his muscles grow tense. Something is bothering him.

"But I've been thinking and came to a realization. I need you to tell me *everything*."

"I—"

"*You* are holding back," he says, turning around to face me. He's got Whipsnap in his hands. I left it in the living area, which I knew was stupid, but I couldn't bring myself to carry a weapon while Luca showed me around the home. "No ordinary hunter could kill Ull. I'm one of the best, and I failed to come close. Not even Ninnis could do it. I know what they planned to do with you. I know about Nephil. And Tarturus. And the blood. The only way I can see you killing Ull is by using a strength greater than your own, which means you are already bonded with the body of Nephil."

He lowers the blade tip of Whipsnap, of my own weapon, toward my stomach. "Which means you brought that monster into *my* home, to *my* children, and if you cannot explain yourself in the next few moments, I will gut you where you stand."

21

I'm surprised at myself when I nearly lunge for Whipsnap. I'm not sure if the desire to claim the weapon is self-defense or merely because I've become so attached to it. I manage to control myself, but Tobias sees the intent hidden in my eyes. His muscles tense in preparation for a fight.

But I'm not Ull, and fighting this man is out of the question. He deserves the truth. I only hope he won't kill me when he hears it.

I raise my hands and step back, trying to think of a way to explain things. But there is no way to dull this news. "It's true," I say. "I am bonded to the flesh of Nephil."

Whipsnap's blade moves closer.

"But," I say quickly. "That was a long time ago. At least a year. I think. It's hard to tell down there."

"I should kill you," he says. "You're dangerous."

"Not anymore," I say. "There was a time when that small part of Nephil fought for control. Along with my own dark side.

You must know what that's like."

"And I know it cannot be defeated," he says. "The hunter is always there, urging me to kill."

"Like now," I note.

He glances down at Whipsnap, then back to me. "Do not try to trick me."

I slowly lower my hands, palms open, and assume a relaxed, non-threatening posture. "If there was any hunter left in control of me, never mind Nephil, do you think I could stand here, with a weapon aimed at my stomach, and speak to you?"

"How?" He asks. "How is it possible? The hunter is part of you. It is closer to the surface with the broken, but it is a part of every human being on Earth. You cannot bury it."

"You can," I say.

"*How?*" His voice is urgent and I sense he is close to acting if I don't give him a convincing answer.

"With help," I say.

He steps closer. "Who?"

"Xin."

His eyes go wide, but he does not strike. "Xin? Why would that monster help you?"

"It wasn't his intention when he found me," I say. "He meant to kill me."

"And become a hunter in reward."

I nod. "He nearly succeeded, but then… Nephil. He took control. Nearly killed Xin. But together, in my mind, we locked Nephil away, along with my hunter personality."

"You left him to die, I hope," he says.

"No," I say. "That is what a hunter would do. Not me. I saved him. And when Behemoth came, he saved me, and hid me from the other hunters."

Whipsnap slowly lowers to the floor. "You faced Behemoth, and survived?"

"Thanks to Xin, yes."

"And you spared his life?"

"That's what I said."

He sits on the edge of a cot, slowly shaking his head. "This is unheard of, you realize. The hunters do not know mercy."

I grin. "Well, at least three of them do now."

"Three of them?"

"I have sparred Ninnis. And Kainda as well."

He laughs at this. "Do not expect the same kindness in return from those two. You may yet find that letting them live was a horrible mistake."

His words ring true. I turn my gaze to the floor.

"But," he says, "I find your story of mercy inspiring. It is a new kind of strength. Perhaps it will be enough to undo the evil already set in motion."

He tosses Whipsnap to me and I catch it, feeling more confident with it in my grasp.

"Xin's help alone wouldn't be enough to chain the will of Nephil," he says.

"It was just his body," I say. "Not his spirit."

"A spirit they believe you are strong enough to contain. Which means you are a person of uncommon strength. Xin might have aided, but I believe the true strength came from you.

From the power instilled in you at birth."

I remember that he witnessed the moment of my birth. He saw the light and the cracking of the ice.

"When we fought," he says. "I haven't missed my target in a very long time. Em is even more of a marksman than I. How were you doing it?"

He's no longer threatening me, but still deserves answers. "Put out your hand."

He furrows his brow in confusion, but complies. I focus on the small amount of moisture in the air, mostly from our breath, and bring it together. It's still imperceptible until I use the cold to bind the water together as ice crystals, forming a perfect snowflake. He catches sight of the flake as it falls and is guided down by small gusts of wind. The snowflake drifts back and forth, and it gently settles down in the palm of his hand.

"You did this?" he asks, watching the flake melt into a small bead of water.

"I don't understand it fully," I say. "But at the moment of my birth, I was bound to the continent, and the continent to me. We are one and the same. I can control the air, earth and water, though the effort leaves me severely weakened."

"Then my arrows—"

"Deflected by the wind. Which is how I killed Ull. Fueled by the recent bonding with Nephil, I turned Ull's own arrow against him. The same effort now would leave me exhausted."

As this last bit of truth exits my mouth, I suddenly remember that I have just as many questions for Tobias, as he does for me, and I am entitled to some answers. "Luca," I say, snapping his attention back up to me. "He's…me?"

A slow nod.

"How is that possible?"

"For thousands of years, the Nephilim have perfected the dark art of manipulating life. The thinkers conjure ideas for new creations. The gatherers collect the raw materials. And the breeders are used to give life to new monsters by altering the feeders before they are born."

I remember the copy of my mother and a sudden fear clutches my throat. "Raw materials?"

"Samples of living things. Flesh. Blood. Hair."

"Do they…kill the…"

"You have encountered a creation you recognized?" he asks.

"Ninnis trapped me in a feeder pit. I escaped it not long before you found me. But the first feeder that hatched. It was—" Tears brew in my eyes. "—my mother."

Tobias approaches and kneels before me. He's looking at my eyes, but not into them. His attention is drawn to my tears. "You were telling the truth," he says. "Hunters cannot shed tears. The creature you met was not your mother."

"I know," I say. "But to create it they had to—"

"Ahh," he says, understanding my concern. "The Nephilim are paranoid about being discovered. They prefer to strike like the tiger—with overwhelming force and only when the target is unaware. They leave as little evidence of their presence as possible. If a person is taken, they are returned with little memory of the event. It's only on rare occasion that someone is killed or taken, and that only happens when there is a logical explanation for how it could have happened."

"Like me wandering off into a storm at night."

"Exactly," he says.

"Do they visit the outside world often?"

Tobias frowns. "Gatherers do all the time. They are some-times seen as flashes of light, or remembered as owls, but in general, their passing goes unseen, or at most misunderstood. But the gathered materials are brought here to be used in Nephilim experiments."

"Like Luca?"

"When news of your strange birth reached the warriors, I was ordered to take you. But by that time, the station had been aban-doned and you had been taken away." He opens a desk drawer and takes out a small wooden box. "I searched the station, discov-ered your room and found this." He opens the box and reveals a comb. A few strands of short white hair are caught between the teeth.

My hair.

My baby hair.

"I took several strands back to them. Years later, they pre-sented Luca to me. I was to raise him as my son in preparation for bonding with Nephil. It was an honor beyond comparison, one for which Ninnis believed himself deserving. But as Luca grew older, their tests revealed that whatever made your birth special had not been duplicated in Luca. They ordered him destroyed. By my hand. I took him to Behemoth, intending him to be a sacrifice to the guardian of Tartarus."

He pauses. I cannot take the silence. "And?"

"And I intended to kill him. I was a loyal servant." He meets my gaze. "Em stopped me."

"How?"

"I had not noticed she and Luca spending time together. Hunters don't pay attention to such things. She wasn't just playing the part of a sister. In her mind, she *was* his sister. And since Hunters are only allowed one child, the way it changed her could not be predicted, nor could her passionate defense of his life. She nearly killed me."

"Why didn't she?"

"Luca. The boy was not corrupted, like us. And to him, even with all my flaws, I was still his father. Like you, Luca understands mercy. It was the first of many chinks in the armor of this hunter."

He sees me watching him and stiffens his posture, embarrassed by his openness. "We fled, hiding in the underworld at first, and then headed toward the surface. Only I knew of this place, so we came here. Have been here since. The day you returned and dug through the ice, Luca was here, right beneath you."

The glut of information is overwhelming me, but there is one more question I need answered. "Are there others? Like Luca? Like me?"

"They tried several times," he says with a sad nod. "They used many different mothers, both human and breeder. They combined you with animals. And Nephilim. Abominable creations."

"Are any of them—"

He winces, knowing the question I'm about to ask, and in that action, I know the answer before he speaks it.

"—still alive?"

"Some," he says. "Those with promise were spared."

I'm about to ask who and what they are, but Tobias cuts me off. "Thinking of such things is of no use to you or anyone else."

"But—"

"Such dark thoughts will only set you back. If the future is to be brighter, you must not focus on the darkness."

"Okay, Yoda," I say

His confused look makes me smile. "It's from a movie."

"A movie?"

I remember how old he is, not to mention where he's been most of his life. "Forget it. I understand what you're saying, but it's going to be hard to ignore while living with Luca."

He stands. "That's why we're going to give you something else to think about."

I raise an eyebrow and think about making a Spock joke, but keep it to myself.

"This power you have—your connection to this continent. With it, you could stand against an army."

"I'm not sure I can do that."

He places a hand on my shoulder like my father used to. "You will not stand alone." He opens the door. "Get some rest today. Tomorrow, we start your training."

22

Three weeks later, I wake to the sound of laughter. It is a noise that has become familiar again—so much so that I can identify the source and cause. The high pitched laugh belongs to Luca. But it's mixed with the occasional playful growl from Em.

A tickle fight.

Em will eventually allow Luca to get the upper hand. Being scrawny and highly ticklish, the boy doesn't stand a chance. I should know. But Em is a good sister. The kind I always wanted. I suppose, the kind I have now.

Though she's not really an older sister. Neither of us really knows our exact age anymore. The underworld can do that. Physically, I'd place both of us around fifteen. Maybe sixteen. But because she lived underground for so much of her youth, she's probably closer to twenty surface years old. Time is a screwy thing.

A high pitched squeal reveals the battle has grown more intense. Realizing a return to sleep will be impossible, I sit up on my bed with a groan. My body aches. Every inch of it. Tobias has been training me, physically, mentally and emotionally every day since my arrival. At first it reminded me of soccer practice. Mindless exercises. Running. Lots of running. But then he combined the physical activity with mental. While I ran I had to will a snow flake to follow me. That simple task made the running nearly impossible. After a week I could complete the run while moving a trail of snowflakes behind me.

At first, I thought he was insane, but as the days passed I understood that he was conditioning my body and mind so that I could use my abilities without getting physically exhausted. Creating a chain of snowflakes doesn't sound like much, but the effort over time takes a brutal toll. When I had mastered the snowflake-chain run, Tobias ran with me. He would talk about my family, my past. He brought up a number of sensitive topics that tore emotional wounds like rusty nails—dirty and jagged.

Here was my weakness. My emotions. I cling to the past, to my parents and my childhood. Instead of facing what is in front of me, I'm always looking back. Always unprepared. Always hurt. Wounded. Sensitive.

I argued that these were the things that separated me from the hunters, but Tobias explained that it was my mercy and love that made me different. The rest just made me afraid. "It's possible to be brave, even fierce, and still be good," he told me. After deciding he was right, I embraced the exercise and fought to purge the demons that filled me with a fear strong enough to control me and give my enemies an advantage. So we pushed harder, exploring the current limits of my abilities.

And it was through this week-long push that we made a discovery. There are many things I can do on a grand scale that do not severely drain me. I can conjure a snow storm, the katabatic winds or roll in a fog from the ocean. These are all natural phenomena and can be accomplished with little effort. But moving a trail of snowflakes behind me, for miles, is *not* natural. Nor is opening a path through the earth, creating a snow storm underground or using the wind to jump higher, to stick a landing or deflect weapons. The unnatural uses of my abilities are created by my will alone and are not aided by the landscape; they are in defiance of it. As a result, the unnatural uses of my connection with the continent are where Tobias is now focusing his attention.

The strain is worse than ever.

And today will be the worst day yet.

The door bursts open. I reach for Whipsnap, but my aching body is slow and the intruder is upon me in a flash.

"Solomon!" Luca shouts. "Save me!"

The boy is all smiles. His blond hair—my blond hair—floats around his head, held aloft by static electricity. No doubt from hiding beneath a blanket. But that did him little good and now he's seeking an ally. He normally runs for Tobias, who turns the tickling on Em. But today, he has come to me.

He's gripping the back of my shirt. I can feel his quick breaths on the back of my neck. His breath smells like fish, which is our staple breakfast, lunch and dinner. Tobias once brought home a seal and I refused to eat it out of respect for Gloop and his pod. After I explained this, Tobias hasn't brought home another seal.

Em steps into the doorway, her fingers clenched and ready to tickle. She's wearing a long yellow T-shirt with a Nike swoop that belonged to Aimee once upon a time. It hangs down to her knees. She looks pretty in it, but I feel no attraction to her. Not like I do when I think of Mira...or Kainda. Maybe it's because of her relationship with Luca, the little me, but the bond between us is more like family than anything else.

Though it is a bond that is still being formed, hence her pausing at the threshold to my room.

Luca giggles behind me, shifting his weight back and forth in anticipation of the impending attack. But I'm not sure it will come. Em and I look at each other. We're both hunters, or were, and this kind of face off usually ends in battle, perhaps with one or the other being killed. Our eyes meet and for a moment, we're sizing each other up.

But then she smiles.

And attacks.

And I'm sandwiched between a brother and sister who are laughing and trying to tickle each other. For a moment, I'm lost. I've never been in this situation. I was an only child. I had no friends that played like this. Then someone's fingers find my armpit and I burst out laughing. The attack comes from both sides as the former enemies unite against me. I fall back on my bed, doing my best to fend off the tickling attack, but failing miserably. If hunters used this technique in battle I would be defenseless.

I'm saved by a knock at the door. Tobias clears his throat and

Em, Luca and I separate and sit up, doing our best to look serious and attentive (something that Tobias often requires), but he's hiding a smile too.

"Get dressed and eat your breakfast. Both of you," he says to Em and me. "We're going to step things up today."

"Can I go today?" Luca asks.

"Not today," Tobias replies.

"But—"

Tobias tilts his head with a frown. "It's too dangerous. You know that."

"Then train me," the little boy says, showing his fists. "I want to fight the monsters, too. Like Solomon!"

Tobias sighs. "When you're older. For now, you must stay here. No more arguing." He leaves the room before the little boy can complain.

Luca crosses his arms with a huff.

"I'll train you," I say.

His eyes brighten. "You will?"

A quick glance at Em reveals she thinks this is a bad idea. I smile at her and turn back to Luca. "I will. Lesson number one, tickle defense."

I grab the boy and start tickling. His laughter breaks the tension. When I let up for a moment, he leaps out of the bed and runs from the room. I hear his feet padding down the hallway. "You can't catch me!"

I look at Em and she's smiling at me. "What?" I ask.

"You're a good brother," she says.

I shrug. "It's easy to be a brother to yourself."

"I wasn't talking about Luca," she says, and then punches my shoulder. "I was talking about me."

"Thanks," I say, and then punch her back.

Before she can hit me again, I leap from the bed and head for the door.

"I'll get you later," she says. "Father had me collecting rocks and I think he means for me to throw them at you today."

I pause in the hallway and lean my head back into the room. "For real?"

She nods with a fiendish grin.

"Be merciful," I say.

"Nah," she says, her smile widening. "That's your thing. Besides, I haven't practiced on a moving target in a while." Her laughter chases me down the hallway, but an hour later I learn that she wasn't joking.

23

The first rock that hits my leg feels like a hard punch. Justin would call it a Charley Horse. I'm not sure why. Never did look that up. But it hurts and slows me down. I'm just glad Em is throwing rocks instead of knives. Still, she *could* hold back a little.

One hundred five.

But I guess that would defy the point. I'm not training for the circus, I'm training for battle, in a makeshift ice arena hidden from view by what appear to be naturally formed walls of ice. You'd have to be standing on the edge to see us inside. A month ago, the fight we're now simulating was real, and I lost. If not for Em seeing my shock of blond hair and deflecting Tobias's arrow, I'd be dead.

One hundred ten.

Might be now, too, if Tobias hadn't replaced the razor sharp metal barbs at the tips of his arrows with cloth-wrapped stones. When the first of those strikes my shoulder, I shout in pain, wondering if something is broken or dislocated. But I can still move the limb.

One hundred fifteen.

Tobias has forbidden me from using my powers for the first two minutes of the fight. Sometimes I'll need to face enemies even when I'm tired and beaten, he said. Makes sense, I suppose, but I was tired and beaten when I got out of bed this morning.

As a hunter I should be able to dodge some of their attacks, but both have remarkable aim and seem to sense where I'm going to move next. I wonder if this is Tobias's way of also teaching me what I am without my powers—not much. An average hunter. A useless—

One hundred twenty!

The arrow headed for my gut shoots wide as a gust of wind pulses in front of me.

A storm forms above us. It's an easy thing to do and doesn't tax my body or mind. All the elements were already there, ready to form on their own. I just gave them a nudge, and asked them to be harsh.

The temperature drops. I can't feel it myself, but I see Tobias and Em react to it for a moment. The chill will sap their energy just as using my unnatural abilities steals mine. This is just the first phase of my counter attack.

But my opponents don't let up. The stones and blunt arrows keep coming. And with each deflected shot, I feel my energy wane. So I try something new. Rather than focus on countering each individual attack, I pull the wind down, and around me. The effort is tiring, but not nearly as much as my previous efforts. A cyclone forms around my body, obscuring me from view and deflecting every single stone and arrow they throw at it. For the moment, I'm safe.

I hear Em shout a battle cry.

But that's all. I just hear her. My defense has blinded me as well.

Her face bursts through the wall of spinning snow, her hands reaching out for me. But then she's gone, yanked away and thrown by the wind. I hear her shout out in pain.

The cyclone bursts.

The wind stops.

And I turn around, looking for Em, terrified that I've hurt her. "Em, are you okay?"

A fist answers my question.

I stagger back, blood dripping from my nose.

I see a stone flying toward me, and I manage to deflect it with a gust of wind.

"You can't be distracted by worries or concerns while in battle," Tobias says.

I channel a long gust of wind behind me, knowing that Tobias is going to shoot me, but not knowing when or where. The arrow zips past my shoulder and buries itself in the snow. But the effort has worn me out. I've lost my advantage.

Or have I?

I'm surrounded by stone and arrows.

They're larger and heavier than snowflakes, but the principle is the same. I've trained for this. I can do it.

I leap away, using the wind to put some distance between Em and I. She's a brutal close-combat fighter, which is why she prefers the knives. And why I prefer to be far away.

I glance to Tobias. He's reaching back for another arrow. Em's taking aim with her stones.

Let them come, I think. I've been thinking defensively so far. It's time to turn things around, literally. The effort might exhaust me, but I want to win this fight.

Em and Tobias time their next strikes so that rock and arrow will arrive simultaneously, forcing me to dodge one, but not the other.

I dodge neither.

Instead, I stand my ground, thurst my hands out toward the projectiles and with matching bursts of wind, force them back the way they came.

Tobias reacts quickly, rolling to the side as his own arrow passes over him.

Em is not as fast and takes the rock hard on her chest. It knocks the air from her lungs and knocks her over. This leaves Tobias for the moment. He's back on his feet, nocking another arrow, but I don't give him the chance to use it.

There are seven arrows lying on the ground. And thirteen stones. But all at once, they return to the air, hovering around me. And I direct them, one by one, toward Tobias. A grin spreads on my face as I watch him duck, dodge and weave to no avail. Not every shot finds its target but enough do. *How does it feel?* I think.

Tobias stumbles when a stone strikes the side of his leg, but he does not fall. The rules of the fight were simple. The first side to be knocked down wins. Em fell, but to end this fight, I need to also make Tobias fall. Unfortunately, he's fast and tough. But I don't stop. I reach out to the stones and arrows I'd already thrown and keep the barrage going. Sooner or later he'll—

Crunch, crunch, crunch.

Em is back up! I had assumed she would stay down, but I have to knock *both* of them down to win. As long as one of them is still in the fight, they're both in the fight. I pull Whipsnap free from my belt for the first time in this fight, but Em is already inside my strike zone. She catches my weapon with both hands, leaps into the air and places her feet against my chest. *She's using my own ninja move against me!* I think, as I'm pulled down and kicked up into the air.

A gust of wind slows my descent and allows me to land on my feet, but Em has stripped me of my weapon, and the fight is beginning to wear on me. I've come a long way with Tobias's guidance, but the two of them are still more than a match for me. As was Xin. But why? I beat Ninnis in the past. Kainda, too. Countless creatures and cresties. And I *killed* the giant Ull. What's different?

Ull, I think. *My Ull.* I've lost that savage energy. But he is dangerous. He would kill Tobias and Em. He would—

A stone strikes my shoulder.

Distraction is your enemy.

A second stone finds my knees, stabbing pain up into my gut and knocking me onto my knees.

Forget everything.
Focus on the fight.
Not on yourself.

Not on who you're fighting.

An arrow grazes my forehead, knocking me back.

My back arches toward the snow. My head hovers just inches from the ground. The only thing keeping me up is the fact that my legs, which are positioned beneath me, don't bend that far.

In that moment, with defeat just inches away, I realize something. Tobias was wrong about one thing. I think about the photo in my pouch. I picture Mira's face. My smile next to hers. I relive the moment. My parents talking in the front seat. The music playing on the radio. The smell of our car and aftertaste of Aimee's chocolate chip cookies in my mouth. The memory gives me hope, and in hope, I find strength.

With a shout, I pull myself back up and thrust my hands out. The katabatic winds rush past me, pulsing at one hundred fifty miles per hour. It lasts just a moment, but that's all it takes to knock Em and Tobias to the ice and sending them rolling to the other side of the make shift arena.

My head sags. I can barely move. But I've won. And I didn't pass out, which is a bonus.

Clap, clap, clap.

Applause?

It's not coming from Em or Tobias. They're still on the ground, and looking for the source of the noise, too.

"Well, well, well," says a voice that fills me with dread. "That certainly explains a lot."

It takes a massive effort, but I manage to turn my head up. I see him at the lip of the pit, looking down at me with a rotted smile. Ninnis.

He found me.

Oh no…

He found *us.*

24

Under normal circumstances this situation wouldn't be that bad. Tobias and Em are both highly skilled hunters. Their skills combined with my abilities would be more than enough firepower to take care of Ninnis. But I've just used the last of my energy to defeat Tobias and Em, and through that effort have pummeled their bodies as well. They'll no doubt recover faster than I will, but Tobias's arrows are dulled and Em's knives are rocks. Still, if we can recover, maybe there is hope.

"Nothing to say little Ull?" a new voice says, removing any shred of hope.

Kainda steps up next to Ninnis, gripping her hammer. She appears healthy and strong, no doubt healed of her wounds by Nephilim blood.

As expected, Tobias and Em regain their feet and shake off my last attack. Were it a real fight, they would still have won. I'm all but defenseless right now.

Without a word, Tobias nocks an arrow, takes aim and lets it fly.

Neither Kainda nor Ninnis flinch. The arrow strikes Ninnis's shoulder. He twitches from the impact, but the arrow bounces to the ground. It will leave a bruise. Nothing more.

Ninnis looks at his shoulder with a smile. "You're going too easy on the boy. He excels when the danger is real." He looks at me. "Isn't that right, Solomon?" He speaks my name with venom.

Em and Tobias stand their ground, waiting for the inevitable fight. At close range, Em could probably do some damage with the few remaining stones she has. And Tobias's bow still has the blades at either end. But as Tobias takes a step toward me, he limps.

I've injured him.

Maybe Em, too.

What was I thinking? I could have killed them!

I look up at Kainda, hoping to see a glimmer of change. I saved her and then spared her life. Even expressed feelings for her! She meets my eyes with a cold blooded stare. A killer to the core.

Tobias was right. I shouldn't have let her live. What good is mercy if it leads to evil?

Maybe if I delay things, the father and daughter team will stand a chance. They have trained to fight as a pair. If they can regroup… "How did you find me?"

"Tracking you took some time, I'll admit," Ninnis said. "You covered your tracks well. But finding you here, in your little arena. Well, that was easy." He smiles in a way that says his next words will cause us pain.

I see Kainda's muscles flex. She knows what he's about to say and that it will spur a response. I realize what he's going to say a moment before he speaks and I nearly throw up.

"It didn't take much," Ninnis says. "With a little...coaxing, the boy was happy to tell me where you were. But don't worry, I left him with Pyke and Preeg." The glint in his eyes says that this is, in fact, something to be very worried about.

"Monster!" Tobias shouts, charging forward despite his wounds.

Em follows his lead, heading for Kainda. She's half her size, but faster and can attack from a distance. Still, in her current condition and without her knives, I do not expect her to survive the encounter.

And there is nothing I can do!

I try to stand, but my legs are numb.

I reach out to the continent, willing the wind to help, but the effort brings blackness to my vision. At the brink of unconsciousness, I give up.

I am helpless.

All I can do is watch.

Tobias lets his last two arrows fly. Ninnis dodges one, but the other strikes his leg. Had they been actual arrows, Ninnis would have been incapacitated. Instead, he's just angry. With a roar, Ninnis leaps into the arena.

Kainda follows, raising her hammer above her head and leaping for Em.

The raw ferocity on display by Ninnis and Kainda increases my sense of hopelessness. They are in top form, hunters about to make a kill. Em and Tobias aren't just wounded, they're emotionally compromised. Like me. Distracted by the potential fate of poor little Luca.

Em lets a barrage of rocks fly at Kainda, but the Amazonian-like woman simply raises her large stone mallet in front of her face, blocking any strikes that might knock her unconscious, and takes the body blows without flinching. Em dives under her, as Kainda lands, striking the snow where Em stood a moment before. I actually feel the ground shake beneath me from the impact.

Em rolls to her feet, and stands, now weaponless. "Why are you doing this? We were friends once!"

"Hunters do not have friends," Kainda says, before beginning a series of attacks that puts Em on the defensive.

Tobias and Ninnis meet at the center of the arena, but Tobias gets the upper hand right away. His razor edged bow gives him a reach that Ninnis cannot penetrate. But it quickly becomes apparent that Ninnis is simply playing with the man, dodging each strike easily while his opponent wears himself out. My father called the fighting style the rope-a-dope, a boxing technique used by Muhammad Ali when he would assume a defensive position against the rope and let his opponent pummel him until exhausted and making mistakes. That's when Ali would strike and bring a quick closure to the match.

That's what I see happening here, but there is no way to warn Tobias.

With a deep breath, I put my hands beneath me and push. My arms shake, but I manage to reach a kneeling position. The effort has set my head spinning, but it's progress. I take another breath and prepare to stand.

And that's when it happens.

Kainda's long leg penetrates Em's defenses and catches her in the stomach. Em crumples in pain with a shout.

The sound of his daughter's pained voice pulls Tobias's attention away from Ninnis for just a moment. But it's all the old man needs.

Ninnis steps inside Tobias's swing and catches his arm. Two quick elbows later, Tobias stumbles back, his face covered in blood from his nose and forehead.

"Father!" Em yells, leaping back to her feet. She tries to run to his aid, but Kainda catches her jacket and throws her against the hard, icy wall of the arena. The wind is knocked out of her again.

I want to shout at Em and Tobias, and tell them to stop thinking about the other. This is what you warned me about! Stop it! Stop caring! Start fighting! But my efforts to stand keep me silent. With a grunt, I find my feet.

But my efforts are far too little and much too late.

Tobias swings at Ninnis despite being blinded by a curtain of red oozing from his forehead. Ninnis snatches the bladed bow, and pulls Tobias in, kicking him hard in the chest. Tobias loses his grip on his weapon and falls back.

There is no banter. No last words. Ninnis is a hunter and he strikes like one.

Without hesitation.

Without mercy.

And with perfect aim.

He leaps into the air, raising the bow above his head, and with a battle cry that turns my stomach sour, plunges the bow into Tobias's chest. Tobias's body twitches under the impact. Ninnis twists the blade, and the body lies still.

Tobias is dead.

Revulsion helps me find me voice. "No!" I scream.

But there isn't time to mourn Tobias's death. Kainda stalks toward Em where she lies, motionless on the ground. She raises the hammer—a weapon strong enough to crack cresty skulls and shake the very ground. Issuing her own war cry, she brings the weapon down. A loud crunch brings a sob from my mouth.

Kainda picks up Em's limp body and tosses her hard. Her body skids across the area floor and stops fifty feet away.

Motionless.

My surrogate family is dead.

And kidnapped.

And I can't even avenge their deaths. But I have to try.

I bend down, head swirling, and pick up Whipsnap.

As Ninnis walks toward me, I hold the weapon between us. But my shaking hands make the defensive posture just look pitiful.

Kainda remains still, watching with crossed arms and downturned lips.

"I saved you," I say to her. Her frown deepens, but I'm not sure if it's from guilt or shame at needing to be saved.

I face Ninnis. He's just ten feet away. "I saved both of you."

He stops just out of Whipsnap's reach. "Your life is a series of mistakes, Solomon."

When he says my name again, I realize I have an opening to put a wedge between these two. "You've told her then? That you failed to break me? And that your failure resulted in Ull's death?"

I see surprise register on Kainda's face. I turn to her. "*I* killed Ull. Your father covered it up."

Ninnis bares his teeth and a growl enters his voice. "Kainda and I have *both* failed when it comes to you," Ninnis says. "It is a shame we bear together. And it is a shame we will correct together."

"You cannot break me again," I say. I'm not sure if it's true, but I need him to believe it.

To my surprise, he nods, but then says, "I do not need to break you again. I simply need you to give yourself—willingly— to the spirit of Nephil."

"Never," I say.

"Then the boy will be killed."

My stomach tightens. Luca is alive.

"I will give you seven days to reach the gates of Tartarus. You will come, as Ull."

"I'm not Ull," I say.

"Then you must be convincing," he says. "You will give yourself to Nephil. He will break you himself. And the boy will be spared." He grins wide, showing his rotting teeth. "You see? I am not without mercy!"

Filled with rage, I lunge, stabbing Whipsnap toward his chest. But my former trainer is fast. He dodges to the side, and in the time it takes me to blink, there is a sword in his hand. Before I have time to contemplate where it came from, he strikes

Whipsnap with the flat side of the blade. The tip of the sword wraps around Whipsnap. With a tug, he pulls my weapon from my hands and flings it away.

He holds the sword out toward me. Its blade is once again straight and razor sharp. "Meet Strike," he says. "A gift from Enki. And if you do not reach the gates of Tartarus within seven days, Strike will be the source of little Luca's prolonged and agonizing death."

Ninnis becomes a blur. I see a flash as Strike coils itself down to the hilt, which then strikes my head. I fall to the ice, staring up at the blue sky above. Ninnis stands over me and says. "Seven days."

Then he's gone. I can hear his feet on the snow, walking away. Kainda's too. Neither of them speaks. They're just leaving me here, with my dead friends, and a demand I have no choice but to grant. I don't believe Ninnis will spare Luca, but I can't leave the boy. I can't let him be killed. My head lolls to the side and I see Kainda at the top of the arena wall.

She glances back at me, meets my eyes, and shakes her head.

Then she's gone, along with Ninnis, and Luca.

I picture the boy in the darkness of the underworld, surrounded by killers and monsters and remember what I was like as a six year old. The experience might very well break him.

I shout and try to rise. If I could only regain my strength I might be able to stop them before they disappear into the depths. But my body doesn't respond. I can't move. I can't fight.

I can't win, I think, so I do the only thing I can do.

I weep.

25

I don't know if I can move. I haven't tried. The will to act has abandoned me. I've lain in the snow at the bottom of the arena for nearly an hour, watching the sun cut across the sky, feeling its rays burning the exposed skin of my tear-streaked face. I've replayed the events surrounding Tobias's and Em's deaths, and Luca's capture a hundred times, looking for a way things could have been different.

The problem is, I find a solution every time. Had I been stronger. Had Ull still been a part of me. If I'd trained harder. If I'd never come here. If, if, if. There are probably a million "what ifs" that could have avoided this situation.

But none of that matters, because it happened. Tobias is dead, killed by his own weapon after I—the memory of that last blast of wind that sent he and Em flying replays in my mind's eye, over and over. It's the single "what if" scenario that pains me the most. I shouldn't have struck them so hard. I shouldn't have been so focused on winning that I put their lives in jeopardy.

But I did.

And they're dead.

The sound of snow shifting in the distance tears me away from my self-deprecation.

The wind?

Footsteps slowly approach. The wind doesn't walk.

I listen to the footfalls coming closer, but don't move. Maybe it's a polar bear come to put me out of my misery.

Polar bears live in the Arctic, stupid, I tell myself. *This is the* Ant*arctic!*

"Solomon?" the voice is weak. Frail. But I recognize it.

I turn toward the shuffling sound, eyes wide. "Emilie?"

She stands five feet away, clutching an arm and covered in blood.

But alive.

"You're alive," she says, sounding relieved.

"*You're* alive," I respond. "I thought for sure—"

"Me too," she says. "What happened?"

The answer to her question stuns me, so much so that I can't bring myself to say it right away. I force myself into a sitting position. My head pounds for several moments, but then clears.

"Kainda," she says. "She beat me. Kicked me." She's struggling with the memory. "She threw me?"

"She—" Saying the words is hard, not because they're hurtful, but because they're hopeful. And I had given up hope. "She *spared* you."

As I say it, I know it's true. Kainda doesn't let someone live without intending it.

Em looks confused. "She doesn't do that."

She's right. Kainda is a brutal warrior known to hold a grudge and react with swift violence. She is not the forgiving type. But still, here Em stands, injured, but alive.

"You did it," she says.

I tense, believing that she is accusing me for being the cause of Tobias's death. A quick glance in his body's direction confirms his death. The snow around his body is as red as his hair. But Em's words aren't accusatory.

"You got through to her," she says. "Your mercy. It's the only explanation."

"You were friends, you said. Couldn't that be—"

"We trained together. Hunted together. Killed together. She's older than me. Old enough to be my—"

Em falls silent for a moment, but shakes her head.

"Perhaps it was both of us, then?" I propose.

Em reaches down for me and helps pull me to my feet. Her strength surprises me. Not just her physical strength, but the resolve she is showing in the face of her father's death. Perhaps it is the hunter in her that won't allow her to cry by his side, or the need to be strong for Luca. Whatever it is, it is an ability I don't have. And she sees the evidence all over my face.

She scoops some snow into her hands, cups them together and melts it between her palms. She uses the water to wipe away the salty streaks. Her touch stings my burned flesh, but bring focus to my mind. A realization strikes.

"It's not just Kainda," I say.

She pauses. "What do you mean?"

"Ninnis, he…he showed mercy."

Her hands drop away from my face and some of her buried emotions rise up. Without turning to face her father's body, she thrusts a finger toward it, acutely aware of where he lies, and shouts, "You call that mercy? My father is dead!"

"He couldn't let him live," I say. "Kainda would know."

"*Know what?*" Her voice brews with anger and I realize that I better explain quickly or the bond of brother and sister formed between us might be broken. And I'm going to need that bond in the coming days. We both will.

"That he's different. It's subtle, but it's there."

"Where is it, Solomon?" She's still shouting. Tears bead at the corners of her eyes. "Where?"

"He gave me seven days to return to Tartarus. I'm to give myself up to Nephil in exchange for Luca's life."

She gasps. "You can't."

"I must."

"Nephil will kill *everyone*, including Luca."

"I can't leave him. The point is, Ninnis gave me seven days."

She stares at me, confused.

"The journey from here to Tartarus, in my condition, and knowing the way, will take four days at most. He's given me three extra days."

"For what?"

I look at Tobias's body and she understands.

"To mourn," I say. "To bury the dead. To say goodbye."

It is an act of mercy so subtle that it could easily be missed or explained away, and while I do not expect him to repeat it, or go back on his promise to kill Luca if I do not show, it is shred of hope I will cling to.

I walk on stiff legs to where Whipsnap was flung and pick up my weapon. "We're going to bury your father. We're going to bury him today. Right now. Tonight we'll rest. Tomorrow we'll begin the journey to Tartarus."

I don't question whether or not Em is coming. As much as I'd like her to remain behind, and safe, nothing short of breaking her legs could keep her here.

"Why not rest longer?" she asks. "Regain your strength."

"That's exactly what I intend to do."

"How?" she asks.

"We're going to make a stop along the way," I tell her. "To see a friend in Asgard. And in the meantime, I need you to tell me about the ones who helped Tobias escape with Luca. We are going to need all the help we can get."

She nods, shakes with a chill, and heads for her father's body.

I follow close behind, feeling bad for my lie of omission. While it's true that I'm going to see a friend, it is not for strength. It is for a clear conscience. I need to see Aimee again, to apologize and…to say goodbye.

26

It takes us three hours to bury Tobias. Most of that time is spent carrying his body back to Clark Station One. Digging a grave proved impossible—the ice is thick and dense—so I used my abilities to carve out a six foot deep hole. We wrapped him in a blanket along with his bow and arrows. I used the wind to carry him down into the grave, where he now lies.

We stand there, side by side, Emilie and I, staring down at the body. I've been to four funerals in my life, for each of my grandparents. I remember the words spoken at each one—comforting words, often about being reunited in the afterlife. None of it seems appropriate now, so I stay silent. Em has never been to a topside funeral before, so the ritual will probably just confuse her. There is one part I always appreciated, though. The prayer. Speaking to God. Asking Him to accept the spirit of the deceased into Heaven. A better place. Certainly better than here. Tobias deserves as much.

I bow my head, close my eyes and whisper a prayer to God.

"I don't know much about you, but I know a lot about Tobias. He was a good man. He gave his life in defense of innocence. And he was an enemy of the Nephilim, who, if demons are real, and you are real, are your enemies, too. Give him a new home, please. A better home."

Em's fingers find mine and we grip each other's hands.

"Protect Luca, wherever he is. Keep him safe and never let him doubt that we are coming for him. Protect Em, and me, as we attempt to get him back."

With my thoughts on the task before us, I say, "If possible, turn Kainda to our side, and…" My next words feel wrong for a moment, but then I remember that there is plenty of smiting in the Bible. God will understand. "Destroy our enemies. Kill them all. Please. Amen."

I open my eyes and find Em looking at me, her face wet with tears already wiped away.

"What were you doing?" She asks.

"Praying," I say. "It's something people do at funerals. When we bury the dead."

"But who were you talking to?"

"God," I say.

Her eyes scrunch tight. "You can talk to God?"

I shrug. I'm really not sure. "I thought it was worth a try."

"The Nephilim don't like God," she says. "We weren't allowed to talk about it."

"Well," I say, "You are now." I reach my hands out over the ice grave. "Goodbye Tobias."

"Goodbye, father," Emilie adds.

I close my hands together and the grave fills with ice.

Em lets out a long sigh. "I'll get my knives."

I dip my head in agreement. Neither of us ever intended on resting. Our bodies are trained to recuperate while on the move. We'll stop along the way, but the journey itself will rejuvenate us. We take nothing but the essentials and our weapons. We will hunt for food. I will try to expand my powers further in the way that Tobias wanted me to learn. And we will learn to work together.

Twenty minutes later, we take a last look back at Clark Station One, the place of my birth and Em's home for the past few years. On the outside it's nothing more than a small rise in the ice. But inside, there are countless good memories for both of us.

"Will we ever see it again?" She asks.

I suspect that I never will, but I manage to say, "We'll get Luca back. You can return together." The words are hollow. At least four hunters know about this place. We can never return. Not for long, at least. Unless, that is, those four hunters are killed.

As we enter the cave system in the mountain above Clark Station One, I look at the array of knives covering Em's belt and the crisscrossing harness strapped over her chest. She certainly brought enough knives to finish the job. And if all we were facing were the four hunters, maybe we'd have a chance. But when we reach the gates of Tartarus, there will be an army waiting for us. We won't just have hunters to deal with. Nephilim of every shape and size will gather in expectation of Ull's bonding with Nephil. Not to mention Behemoth.

We're both dressed for the underworld, wearing a minimum of clothing so that we might squeeze through the tight cracks. Em's body is more muscular than I expected. And she moves through the tunnels like fluid. She sets an impressive pace, like her father would have, and drives us deep, toward Asgard.

After a full day's travel, we pause, just an hour's hike from our goal. We decide to rest for a bit, just in case we meet resistance in Asgard.

"We will be noticed right away," she says, leaning back against the stone wall of the small alcove in which we have hidden.

She's right, of course. Even if our faces weren't recognizable, our streaks of normal colored hair will brand us as innocents right away.

"They still believe I am Ull," I say. "Bonded with the body of Nephil. They won't dare attack me."

"And me?"

"I'll—I'll say you're my wife."

Em laughs at this. Her smile is refreshing. "Your wife?"

"I was offered Kainda already. I turned her down."

"And she let you live?"

"You, too," I remind her.

"Fine."

I can tell she's not thrilled about the idea, but it will work. At least long enough for us to get in and out, assuming we don't run into the Nephilim hierarchy. I suspect they are already en route to the gates of Tartarus.

"But we still need to do something about our hair," she says.

She draws a knife from her belt and moves closer to me.

"What are you doing?"

"Just sit still." She looks over my hair. "Huh."

"Huh, what?"

"You have more blond hair than you did the day we met."

"You mean the day you almost killed me."

She grins. "Hey, I saved you, remember?" And before I can stop her, she puts the knife up to her opposite palm and draws the blade across. Blood flows.

I take her arms. "What are you doing?"

She rubs her hands together, smearing the blood. "Trust me," she says.

When I let go, she takes her bloody hands and runs them through my hair. The metallic smell of her blood, so close to me, makes me uncomfortable, but I understand what she's doing. She repeats the process several times until my hair is once again stained fully red, the way Ull's should be.

After finishing, she lets me wrap her hand. I'm no doctor, but I've read a few first aid manuals before. Apparently I do a good job, because when I finish tying the last knot, she flexes her fingers and says, "Perfect."

"You have a two inch slice in your hand," I say. "I don't see how that can be perfect."

"I can still throw and you look like 'Ull, the vessel of Nephil.'" She says the last part with a scary voice that makes me smile.

"What about you?" I ask.

She flips the knife around and places its handle in my hand. I take the knife and place it against my palm. I know she could have done her own hair, too, but this feels right. Like we're blood brothers, or blood siblings at least. But she yanks my hand away and says, "No, stupid, you need to cut my hair off. It's a sign of subjugation to a new husband."

"Oh," I say.

"You didn't know that when you suggested I pose as your wife?"

I shake my head, no. "But now that I do, I like the idea even better."

She punches me hard in the shoulder, much harder than Justin ever could have, but I shrug it off with a laugh. She turns around and says, "Make it quick."

Fifteen minutes later, Emilie is bald. She rubs her hand over her head. She turns around, facing me. "How do I look?"

But I don't really notice how she looks. The missing hair has revealed an image just above her hairline.

She notes my attention. "What?" She quickly becomes insistent. "What is it!"

"A tattoo," I think.

Her face twitches with confusion. "Of what?"

"It's a shape. A pattern really."

"Describe it," she says.

"I doubt it's anything—"

"Describe it." She's getting angry.

"It's two circles, one within the other."

"Which ring is thicker?" she asks.

"The outside ring."

She stares at me, stunned. I have no idea why, but this news has shaken her. "What does it mean?"

She blinks, meeting my eyes. "It means…it means that Tobias was not my father."

"What?" I say. The notion strikes me as ridiculous. "Why?"

She speaks through gritted teeth. "The tattoo is given to people who are taken from the outside world and brought here."

"But I was taken—"

"From Antarctica," she says. "These are people taken from far away. From the other continents. Often from their homes. It doesn't happen often, but when it does, they're marked with a tattoo. The one you described. It means…" She pauses to take a deep breath. "It means I wasn't born here."

The ramifications of this news are like a slap in the face. I take her hand. "Em, it means you have a family. A mother and father. Maybe even brothers and sisters."

She pulls her hand away. "I already had those things."

She's right, of course. I'm now included in that family, but she hasn't thought this through. "A family in the outside world means you have somewhere to go. Somewhere to take Luca. When you get him back, take him to McMurdo. Someone will help you. People are looking for you somewhere. People are—"

She takes her knife from me, slips it back in her belt and stands. "We need to keep moving." She strikes out into the adjoining tunnel that will take us to Asgard, where we will be Ull and wife. If we are recognized there is the potential for trouble, and I must hide the fact that I'm there to see Aimee from anyone that we might come across. So I push Em's harsh reaction from my mind and focus on the task at hand.

Be Ull, I tell myself.

Be ruthless.

Arrogant.

Strong.

Everything I'm not.

We're dead, I think, and I follow Em toward Asgard like a lemming over a cliff.

27

By the time we reach the outer fringes of Asgard, Emilie hasn't said two words. The only way to know you've entered Asgard is the mark of Odin carved into the tunnel wall. Asgard isn't like New Jericho—a city with buildings inside a giant cavern. It is a series of tunnels and chambers carved out of stone beneath a mountain. Ninnis once told me that if the snow ever melted, much of the city would be exposed. Daylight would pour in through windows. Fresh air would seep through the cracks. At the time, I found the notion disagreeable. Now, in the depths of the Earth, I wouldn't mind a little fresh air. It might sweep away the stench of blood and rot that plagues this place.

Em stops and traces her fingers over the mark of Odin—three interlocking triangles—carved into the tunnel wall. She stares at it, remembering.

"I grew up here," she says. "Trained here. With my fath—with Tobias. And Kainda. And Ninnis. Ull, too. I can't say it was a happy place. We had no concept for that word. But when I lived within these walls, the halls of Asgard…" She looks at me. "I felt safe."

I'm not sure what to say to her. Safety is an illusion in the underworld, especially in the presence of the Nephilim, who might randomly decide that you look delicious and eat you. I've never heard of that happening, but they eat their own young, so it's certainly not out of the realm of possibility.

"It was all a lie," she says. "Everything they told me. About my mother. About my father. I never belonged here."

"It wasn't all a lie," I say, surprising myself.

She whips an angry eye toward me, suspicious of why I'd say such a thing.

"Tobias loved you," I say.

"He wasn't my father."

"This kind of thing happens a lot where I'm from. It's called adoption. Children are adopted by a father and mother that aren't biologically related. But they're raised as though they were. And they're loved just the same."

"No one tells the child?"

"It's up to the parents. Some do. Some don't. But the ones that don't usually have a reason. Maybe Tobias was protecting you from something?"

She pulls her hand away from the wall. "My father told me— told everyone—that I wasn't born here, in Asgard. Or any of the cities. My mother, a hunter named Dalia, delivered me deep in the tunnels and died of childbirth complications. Tobias emerged from the tunnels with a baby girl and the story of Dalia's death; no one questioned it. He raised me on his own. I suspect that's why they gave Luca to him, too."

"So he lied about your birth, to you, and everyone else."

She nods slowly. "Outlanders that are deemed unfit are given to Behemoth."

"Is it possible," I say, "that your father and mother were meant to give you to the monster?"

She sniffs and wipes her nose. "I've never heard of a baby bearing the mark being kept."

"Then his lie saved you," I say.

She rubs the tattoo with her hand. "And now?"

"Now," I say, puffing out my chest, "You are married to Ull, scourge of the underworld."

A smile creeps onto her face. "C'mon, scourge, let's get this over with so we can go be eaten like I should have been all those years ago." She turns and steps past the mark of Odin, officially entering the halls of Asgard. "Sorry," she says.

I follow her beyond the mark. "For what?"

"You are my adopted brother," she explains. "As is Luca. I didn't mean to imply that our bond is less than that of blood. I'm proud to call you brother."

I laugh as the tunnel opens up into a grand hall. Pillars carved with the faces of Norse gods stretch down either side. They serve little function other than decoration and intimidation. When I see Ull's face, my stomach turns. The intimidation factor works. But I'm Ull now. So I wipe the growing fear from my face and try to project confidence.

The hall is devoid of life, so I still speak freely. "Em, are there any…customs, any rules about marriage that I should know about?"

Her telltale gasp springs from her mouth. She immediately stops and takes a step back so that she's behind me. "Wives are subservient to husbands," she says. "Not in battle. Then we're all equal. Hunters do not see sexes. But here, in Asgard, and in the other cities, wives must follow close behind their husbands, eyes to the ground."

"What about wedding rings?" I ask.

"Wedding rings?"

"Forget it," I say. Nothing here could be so romantic. Marriage in the underworld is about territory, alliances, spawn and other human needs. But not love. There is no place for love here.

As the pat of bare feet slapping the floor approaches from the branching hallway ahead of us, I realize my last minute lesson in Nephilim marital culture was just in time. He enters the grand hall dressed for the hunt, in skins. His red hair is long, but trimmed, and poufy in a way that reminds me of Kevin Bacon. A chain wrapped around his waist holds two spiked metal balls. I recognize the weapon as a meteor hammer from Justin's ninja books. They were a rare, but deadly weapon used in feudal Japan. Apparently they found a home in the Antarctic underworld as well.

He's still some distance away but walks straight toward us.

"Do you know him?" I whisper.

If Em knows this man and he sees her tattoo, it could cause problems if he realizes the details surrounding her birth are a lie. Actually, she's a fugitive, so there's that, too.

"No," she says. "He must be from one of the other kingdoms. His hair looks Olympian."

At first I think it's strange that she doesn't know him, but Antarctica is as vast as the United States and has several cities spread out across, and beneath it. I never estimated the total population of the underworld. There could be millions.

The thought fills me with dread and I have to work hard not to show it on my face as we approach the stranger.

I meet his eyes, knowing that to do otherwise would be a sign of weakness, something Ull would never do. The man squints at me as we pass, and then he sees Em, head bowed, tattoo exposed.

The man laughs under his breath.

I stop in my tracks and while thinking a panicked, *what are you doing?!* I say, "You find something funny?"

Ull would have never let the laugh pass. I can't, either.

The man turns toward me. He's nearly twice my size and appears to be forty years old, which could mean he's been here for twice that time. A grin forms on his clean shaven face. "When I first saw you I thought it strange that a pup like you could have claimed a wife," the man says. "Then I saw the mark on her forehead." He shakes his head in disgust. "You lower yourself too far, pup."

What would Ull do? "If you call me, "pup," one more time—"

"Pup," the man says.

The attack comes immediately, but it's not from me, or the stranger. Em leaps out from behind me, knives in hand. She lets two fly. The first finds the man's thigh, burying two inches deep into his flesh. He grunts, and dodges the second knife, moving quickly.

In a flash, he's got the meteor hammer spinning like a heli-copter blade. It deflects Em's next two knives.

She won't be able to penetrate his defense.

Ull, however, would have no trouble.

I yank Whipsnap from my belt. The weapon springs to life in my hand. I approach the man with a spin that make it look like I'm going to strike from the side, but instead I thrust the mace end of Whipsnap into the spinning chain. The meteor hammer's chain wraps around Whipsnap's shaft and with a yank, I disarm the man and toss his weapon across the hall.

The action has stumbled the man and his back slaps against one of the hall's columns. Before he can pull himself from it and consider a counter attack, Whipsnap's blade is against his neck. I knick his skin, letting the blood run down the blade so he can see it.

"Do you know who I am, *pup*?" I say with a growl.

He looks me up and down. He has no idea. And he still doesn't care. I see nothing but hatred in his eyes.

Ull might have killed the man by now, but there is only so far I am willing to take this act. "Why are you here, Olympian?"

When he answers, I know Em pegged him right. "I am trav-eling to the gates of Tartarus, to represent my master, Poseidon, who must continue work on the fleet."

I can tell he thinks Poseidon's name will generate some fear or respect in me, but I am Ull, who will one day bear the essence of Nephil and rule over all Nephilim, including Poseidon. I fear no Nephilim.

At least, that's what I'm telling myself. In truth, I'm terrified of the Nephilim. Of this hunter. But I need to keep up the act, for Luca. "And who is it you wait for in Tartarus?"

He scoffs. "You truly are a pitiful one, pup." Even in the face of death, he taunts me. Are all the hunters like this? Like Ull?

I push the blade a little deeper, careful not to accidentally open his jugular. I stop when he winces. "Had you half a brain you might realize who it is you are speaking to."

With a sneer, he says, "Tell me, please, so that I might pass on your name to—"

"I am—Ull!" I shout, drawing the blade back and kicking the man in the gut. When he pitches forward I give him a hard chop to the back of his head and send him to the floor at my feet. "Vessel of Nephil, Lord of the Nephilim. And it is *me* whom you go to see at the gates of Tartarus!"

While he recovers, Em takes my hand and squeezes it.

I'm shaking.

I take a deep breath and speak slowly. "Do you know who *I* am now?"

He nods without looking up, which is a good thing because my hand is still shaking.

"Tell me," I say. "Why shouldn't I kill you?"

As I ask the question, I hope his answer is good, and that he doesn't just go ahead and ask for death.

"I am shamed and forever your servant," he says.

Ull might still run him through, but his answer is enough for me, and useful.

"What is your name?" I ask.

"Doug," he says.

I nearly laugh. *Doug? Really?* It's the most mundane and normal name I've heard in the underworld. Like Norman. Or Chuck. Or Bob. The name also reminds me that he wasn't born here. He wasn't always a hunter. He had a family once. Maybe children. And the menace he feels toward me and everything else was instilled in him by the Nephilim. "Do something for me, Doug" I say.

"Anything."

"The hunters, Preeg and Pyke, do you know them?"

He shakes his head, no. "Then you will learn who they are."

"I will find them," he says.

"They will have a boy with them. A boy who has yet to be broken. Find him and take him, but do not harm him. I would break him myself. Make him my first protégé."

"And if they do not release the boy?" he asks.

I hadn't considered that possibility in my hasty plan, or considered the fact that Luca might now be with Ninnis and Kainda. I give the only answer that Ull could give, "You will give them no choice."

"Understood."

"Now go," I say. "Speak of this to no one. Succeed and I will elevate your status. Fail and I will finish what we began here today." I turn to Emilie. "Fetch his weapon."

She picks up the meteor hammer and hands it to me. I hold the weapon in my hand, feeling the strength of the chain and the weight of the spiked balls. A single blow from this weapon would have been enough to kill me.

We got lucky, I think, and I decide that this visit to Asgard should be brief.

I drop the weapon at my feet and show no fear at the fact that I've just armed the man who moments ago would have killed me. He collects it and stands, his head still downturned. He gives a slight bow, "My Lord," and then heads on his way.

I stand there, watching him leave. When I can no longer see him, I listen. When the sound of his feet fade away, and his scent fades along with it, my legs begin to shake.

"I can't do this," I say, returning to myself.

Em catches me and holds me up. "Where are we going?"

"To my room. You know where they are?"

She gives me a look that says, duh, and adds, "I grew up here, remember?"

She leans me against a column, against the face of Ull of all places, and quickly collects her knives. "For the record, a wife is allowed to defend her husband's honor. Had his wife been present, we would have fought to the death."

My face pales at the thought.

"Don't worry," she says. "I would have won."

With her knives returned to their sheaths, she steps up to me. "Can you walk? Because I can't help you."

I nod and take a shaky step. I push through the weakness and by the time we reach the end of the hall, and enter the next, I have regained the confident strut of Ull. The walls here stretch forty feet high to accommodate the Nephilim warriors. The hallway stretches far to the left and leads to several other hallways, rooms and the grand chamber where I consumed the blood of Nephil. To the right is the curving staircase that leads to the human-sized living quarters, where I hope to find Aimee, and give her something that is more hers than mine—something that will soon do me very little good and might yet save her life. Or at least her soul.

28

I find myself more nervous standing in front of Aimee's door than when I crossed the threshold into Asgard. Seeing her again is going to hurt. Not like it did when I last saw her, when the very sight of her face ripped my surprised Solomon personality back to the surface and buried Ull. This will be different. She's been here for some time now and I'm afraid I'll see horror in her eyes. My first memory after being born is Aimee's smiling face. And I'm terrified the love she normally exudes will have been tainted.

Because of me. I took her. I brought her here. And I'm coming to tell her there will be no escape.

Em looks both ways. She's nervous for a different reason. We're standing in a hallway filled with human sized doors, behind which any number of hunters could lurk. One of the rooms behind us belonged to her and if anyone was going to recognize her, it would be here.

But we haven't seen another soul since Doug.

"What are you waiting for?" She whispers.

"I'm nervous," I reply, and for a moment I feel happy that I have someone I can be honest with about how I'm feeling. It's a rare thing in the underworld. In fact, it's probably unheard of. Of course, the only other person I can be open with lives on the other side of this door.

I knock on the wooden door.

Em shoots me a confused glance. "What are you doing?"

"I'm knocking," I say, but then remember that no one down here knocks. "It's like asking permission to enter."

She shakes her head, twists the doorknob and enters. I follow her in, hoping the rude entry will not make a bad impression. But there is no one inside to impress. The walls are covered in graffiti—symbols and images drawn by hunters and teachers past. But Aimee *has* been living here. I can tell by the collection of topside trinkets she's managed to collect somehow and the red knit blanket on her bed. *How did she get yarn?* I wonder. I run my hand over the red blanket and recognize the texture. It's feeder hair.

There are many other items in the room that I'd like to look through, but time is short. We need to begin the journey to Tartarus soon. But I need to see Aimee! I can't leave her here not knowing what I'm about to do, not knowing that the next time she sees me I might not be myself. I might be Nephil.

My disappointment shows on my face like a lighthouse beacon in the night.

Em takes my hand. "Sorry."

I see a roll of parchment and sticks of charcoal. "I'll leave a note."

"Wait," Em says, her face smiling with revelation. "She's a

teacher, right?"

I nod.

"Teachers spend most of their time in the library. Studying and teaching. It's likely we'll find her there."

I head for the door.

She stops me. "The library is on the other side of Asgard. It's likely we'll run into someone along the way. We didn't have far to travel here, but we'll have to cut through the core of the city to reach her."

"It's a risk we'll have to—" An idea strikes as I glance into the hall and see the door to *my* quarters. I pull Em behind me, rushing for the door. "I have an idea."

There's no hesitation as I enter my room. Memories try to come back and haunt me, but I fight them away. My focus is the clothing laid out on my bed—primarily the cloak made of cresty skin and its cresty-head hood. It's a miniature version of the garb the Nephilim Ull wore and will be instantly recognizable to anyone who sees it. My identity will be revealed, but since no one but Kainda and Ninnis knows I've changed, no one should dare to challenge me, outlander wife or not.

Em sees the cloak and offers three slow nods. "Good idea."

I throw the cloak on, button it over my chest and pull the hood up over my head. The hood still has the cresty's upper jaw and skull, so it's heavy on my head and the teeth bite into my skin. But it has the desired effect. When I turn to Em, she looks uncomfortable. "How do I look?"

"Awful," she says.

"What about you?" I ask. "Do you think your clothes are still here?"

"It's been too long," she says. "They would have been destroyed."

"Then let's go," I say. I lead the way out of the room and toward the human quarters' exit. Halfway there, I freeze.

"What's wrong?" she asks.

"This is where it happened." I say.

Em looks at me, trying to figure out what I'm talking about.

"This is where I killed him. Ull. His head lay here, where I'm standing, with his own arrow buried in his forehead."

Em looks at the stone floor. "It's a good memory."

It's hard to think of an act so violent as a good memory, but I find myself feeling better as I remember how I fought the giant, using my skills as a hunter and my connection with the continent to defeat a monster thousands of years old. It was one of my finer moments, and it allowed Tobias to die a free man.

"C'mon," I say, tugging Em along. "Which way to the library?"

Whispering directions from behind me, Em leads us through the center of Asgard, revealing many of its great halls, which are ornately decorated with sculptures, balustrades and obelisks. The place is like an amalgam of several ancient cultures, with gods from around the world being represented. As I look at a statue of Odin, master of Asgard and father of the Norse god lineage, I realize this whole place is a Nephilim temple built to worship themselves. For the hunters living here, they're constantly reminded that they're living among gods. And for the other Nephilim classes—breeders, gatherers, thinkers and the others—

the fact that they are ruled by the warriors can never be forgotten.

We pass two lone hunters and a group of four gatherers in heated discussion on our way to the library. The hunters meet my eyes, see the cresty skull on my head and then look away, no doubt recognizing me for who I am...or rather, who I'm not. The gatherers either don't notice us at all or don't think twice about our presence.

We reach the entrance to the library and I pause. The doorway is forty feet tall to accommodate the warriors and its stone frame has been covered with an ancient language that I don't recognize. But it's not the doorway that gives me pause.

Em stops next to me and shakes her head. "You know," she says, "for the future Lord of the Nephilim, you're a huge wimp."

I laugh. I can't help it. If anyone saw or heard me, there would be trouble, but her words cut through my nervous tension like Whipsnap through a feeder's belly. "Story of my life," I say, and then we step into the library.

The place, like every other room in this city, is massive. Eighty foot ceilings and untold square footage cause our footsteps to echo. If there is anyone in here, they know we've entered. There are rows of shelves, like any other library, and some of them actually contain books—*human* books from the outside world! I look at them like a kid in an ice cream store. It's been so long since my mind fed on a book. I pull one from the shelf as we pass. It's an old illustrated paperback of *Pilgrim's Progress*, a story that I've actually not yet read. I open one of the pouches attached to my belt and place it inside. I see Em watching me. "What?"

"The gates of Tartarus and the spirit of Nephilim await us in the depths and you're stealing a book."

With a shrug, I say, "I like to read."

We pass through the shelves of books, and enter a world of scrolls, many of which appear to be leather...or more accurately, skin, and I wonder if any of them are human. The monotony of the endless rows discourages me. Finding someone here will be hard, and we don't even really know that Aimee is here.

A light up ahead catches my attention. Most of Asgard flickers from the light of torches. But the light ahead of us is steady. And bright. I squint as we draw closer. Even the brightest crystals underground don't glow so vividly. The source comes into view a moment later. It looks like an oversized light bulb complete with a glass tube and a twisted metal filament inside. It looks very familiar and I search my memory for a reference. I find the answer in a book on Egypt I read when I was eight. The image in my mind comes from the temple of Hathor at Dendera, where a detailed inscription depicts what looks like an over-sized light bulb that looks oddly similar to an early modern light bulb called a Crookes tube. And here it is. The real thing. A giant light bulb attached to a column that rises eighty feet to the ceiling.

The light bulb has engaged my mind so fully that I fail to notice the person sitting beneath it. It's not until she speaks my name, "Solomon?" that I look down and see Aimee, wrapped in a red blanket, with a book in her lap. The scene is so normal that it's abnormal, and I stare at her in silence for a moment. When my thoughts clear, I see her face clearly for the first time in more than a year and realize that I'm not the one who is frightened anymore. Aimee stares up at me, terrified, and with a nervous voice, asks, "Is that…you, Solomon?"

29

I'm confused by Aimee's fear for a moment, but then I remember what I look like. I'm wearing the garb of Ull, my hair is fully blood red and I'm in the presence of a lethal looking hunter with more knives than a shark has teeth. Knowing she must think I've reverted back to Ull, I pull off my cresty hood, and put on a smile.

"It's me," I say. "It's Sol."

She stands quickly. The book and blanket fall to the floor. Before I can blink, her arms are around me, crushing me with a love so strong that I had begun to believe the memory of it was a dream. When she separates, we both have tears in our eyes.

"It's been so long," she says. "I wasn't sure I would ever see you again. And then I heard about the ceremony…" Her hands squeeze my shoulders. "Look at you. You've grown so big! Like your uncles."

My first thought is, she knows my uncles? But then I realize the comment about my size was meant to change the subject. She knows about the ceremony. About the gates of Tartarus. *We'll get to that in a moment*, I decide. "Have you been treated well?"

"Well for a prisoner," she says. "And better than most. I've learned all about the society here. The rules. The things you endured. I have it easy by comparison. If I do as they ask. I study. I teach. And fill my free time how I might have before—reading and knitting, though I do miss baking."

"I remember your cookies."

She smiles. Her kind eyes, broad grin and dark skin reminds me of Mira. "You remember everything."

I look around. There is no trace of another living thing in this library. I see nothing, hear nothing and smell nothing other than old books and dust. "You aren't guarded?"

"They took me to Olympus once. The journey took two weeks, each way, and I got a look at the creatures that live outside. I wouldn't last a day. So there is no concern about me escaping. And there is nothing I can do to them here. I've decided to learn everything I can, and maybe, someday, my knowledge will serve some good."

"You could come with us," I say.

She shakes her head. "I am dreadful in the underground. Claustrophobic it turns out." She looks around. "These giant halls are fine, but in the tight squeezes you hunters use to move about, I'm cryolophosaurus food."

This name isn't familiar. "Cryolophosaurus?"

"The dinosaurs. With the crests on their heads. It's the technical name for them."

"Oh," I say. "I call them cresties. I named one of them Alice.

A thirty foot female."

Aimee cringes. "Sounds dreadful."

"She's dead," I say.

"You?"

I nod. "She was going to eat Kainda."

Kainda's name removes every trace of happiness from Aimee's face. It's easy to see that not everything here has been pleasant.

"Might have been a good idea to let the dinosaur eat that one."

"You're not the first person to tell me that."

"Making friends, are you?" She looks around me, to Em.

I stand to the side. Aimee looks her up and down and then looks back to me. "You've taken a wife?"

Em tries to stifle a laugh, but fails.

"We're in disguise," I explain. "Aimee, this is Emilie. Em, this is Aimee."

Aimee's eyes widen. "Ahh, Emilie. Daughter of Tobias. Bonded to the Nephilim, Tyr."

Em shifts uncomfortably in the gaze of Aimee, who knows a surprising amount about her.

Aimee notices our confused looks and says, "I'm sorry. They've had me creating a chronological history of the house of Odin. You are to be admired, Em. Few have ever broken the bonds and freed themselves from this place. Even fewer have survived as long. Is Tobias with you?"

"Slain," Em says. "By Ninnis."

"Keep away from him," she says. "The man thinks of nothing

but—" Her hand goes to her mouth. "You're going, aren't you? The ceremony. I had hoped you didn't know. That it was a trick of some sort. But it's real. You're to be bonded with Nephil?"

"I have no choice," I say.

"There is always a choice!" She sits down, shaking her head. "Why would you do such a thing? Without you, there's no—"

I crouch in front of her. "Mrs. Clark," I say. The use of her last name brings her eyes to mine. "Ninnis has her brother, Luca. He is unspoiled by this place, with hair as white as the snow."

The news softens her resolve, but she is not yet convinced.

"Tobias took me in, and died as a result. Em is a sister to me now. And Luca, Aimee, he's...he's like a brother to me, but..." I can't think of a way to say this and have it make sense, so I just spill it. "He's me. A little me. Created from hair stolen from Clark Station One."

Aimee's head lowers toward the floor. "I know," she says.

"You *know*?"

"One of many awful secrets I have uncovered in this place. I had hoped you would never find out."

This information stings. That Aimee would keep anything from me feels like a betrayal. I stand and take a step back. "But why?"

"Because of what you are about to do," she says. "Your bond to family has always been strong. I believed they might influence you."

"Influence me?"

"Not all of them are unspoiled," she says, looking me in the eyes. "You would do well to avoid the others."

"If any part of me resides in them, then there might be a chance—"

"No," she says. "Don't even think it."

I decide to drop the subject. The fate that awaits me at the gates makes it a moot point. Unless... "Do you know their names?"

"I will not tell you," she says.

"Is one of them Xin?" I ask.

"*Xin?*" Em says, her voice full of shock and revulsion.

Aimee avoids my eyes.

"Tell me, please!" I knew there was something about Xin worth saving and if it's true, if I'm right, then there might be a shred of hope for me yet. I take Aimee's shoulders in my hands. "Xin saved me, Aimee. And he hid me from the other hunters. Without his help, I would be dead or broken again. Please."

She gives the slightest nod, "He doesn't know. None of them do." She begins crying. "Please don't go. Flee from this place. Go to McMurdo. Go home to your parents. Take Em with you and never think of Antarctica again."

"You know I can't," I say. "My family is growing. There are more allies in the underworld than I ever thought possible. And I will not abandon them here. I will not abandon you."

She takes my hand in hers, brings it to her face and kisses it. She closes her eyes and I feel her tears drip onto my skin. When she opens her eyes again, I'm holding out the gift I needed to deliver, in case I don't come back as myself, or if I never come back.

When she sees it, she lets out a sob so sad that even Em cries a little bit. Aimee takes the Polaroid photo of Mira, her daughter, and me, in a shaky hand. After a moment, she clutches the image to her chest. "Where—where did you get this?"

"I've always had it with me," I say. "It gave me strength when I was alone."

She starts to hand it back, but I push it towards her.

"I'm not alone, anymore," I say with a look back at Em. "You need it more than me."

Having done what I came here to do, I step back and pull the skull hood back over my head and wipe away the tears on my cheeks. "We need to go."

"So soon?" Aimee asks.

"We have four days to reach the gates of Tartarus," I say. "If we're not there in time, Ninnis will kill Luca."

She stands and hugs me. "You have given me a gift more bright than the sun itself. You are *still* a precious boy."

The familiar words, spoken to me by Aimee at my birth and when I was freed from the personality of Ull, brings peace to my heart. Aimee frees me from her grasp and to my surprise, and Em's, wraps her arms around Em and says, "You are a precious girl."

I see Em's face quivering. While Tobias loved her as a daughter, he was never affectionate with her. This is the first physical expression of love, beyond our occasional hand clutch, that Em has ever received, and coming from a motherly person like Aimee, it's almost more than she can bear. I smile when I see the muscles in Em's arms flex as she returns the embrace.

After renewing my promise to one day free Aimee, we leave

the library feeling renewed and emboldened, with a higher sense of purpose beyond simply freeing Luca.

We are the light at war with darkness.

We represent love in a land of hate.

And if we die in its defense, the Nephilim will have lost, and there will be hope for humanity.

30

Our hope disappears when the stench hits. Half a day's journey from the gates of Tartarus, the odor of countless Nephilim and hunters fills the tunnels like an invisible fog. There is no escaping it. The scent of smoke and roasting flesh is mixed with the rancid tang of body odor and refuse. Every step takes us deeper into the stink, and it's not long before I can taste it in my mouth. I'm not sure what's worse anymore, breathing through my nose or through my mouth.

I choose to breathe through my nose because even though the smell is stronger than the taste, the flavor of Nephilim in my mouth repels me. I've tasted it before, when I consumed the flesh of Nephil.

Em stops, resting against the wall of the small tunnel we've been following. We haven't come across another living thing on our journey thus far, nor have we detected anyone following us, but we're sticking to the road less traveled just to be careful. I know Ninnis wants me to arrive as Ull, and show everyone that

I'm willingly giving myself to Nephil, but that doesn't mean he won't have an ambush ready for me. I doubt it, but better safe than sorry.

"You okay?" I ask her. I know she's not tired. We could both continue on at this pace for days.

"I'm just—are you sure about this?" She avoids my eyes. "You launched right into this plan, which might leave you dead or under the control of Nephil, without much thought. I mean, I want to save Luca, too. But I'm starting to wonder if the cost of getting Luca back is too high."

"He's your brother," I say. "He's my brother. He's *more* than my brother."

"What do you mean?" she asks.

"You know...what he is?"

She nods. "Tobias told you?"

"Tobias didn't know everything."

Em steps away from the wall, confusion stitching across her forehead. "Which means I didn't know everything."

"We're connected," I say. "Since I arrived on Antarctica... Luca sees—he can see what I see. Not all the time, but big events. Big emotions. They're like dreams for him, and they don't affect him the way they do me. But he knows. I have no doubt he knows we're coming for him."

Em looks worried. "Do you think he heard? What I said?"

She's afraid to say it again; that maybe rescuing Luca is a bad idea. I don't know how the connection really works, but since I'm not feeling any kind of strong emotion, other than revolt over the smell, I doubt it. "I don't think so," I say, and hope it's true.

Em doesn't say anything, but I know the matter is settled. What kind of people would we be if we didn't risk everything to save our six year old brother? He'd be tortured and killed, or worse, broken and trained to hunt and kill us.

I think leaving a child to that kind of fate would turn my blond hair red again and leave a tarnish on my soul that would remain for the rest of my life.

"Aren't you afraid?" Em asks.

I hold out my hand in response, letting her see it shake. Every step we take closer to the source of the rancid odor, makes it worse. Without the smell, my fear might be manageable. I might be able to put my fate out of my mind for a moment. But the stink is a constant reminder that I'm about to face an army.

On my own.

While Em attempts to rescue Luca.

She takes my hand in hers and squeezes. The shaking abates some and I find my voice. "I'm terrified. I have hidden from this confrontation for a long time and I'm now headed straight toward it. I lost myself once before, and I'm afraid that's going to happen again. Death would be preferable."

Her face becomes that of a hunter's. "If it comes to that..."

She'd kill me. She'd prevent me from becoming Nephil. I have no doubt she would do it, and it gives me comfort. "Thanks."

"Let's go," she says, stepping away.

"If it happens," I say. "If Nephil takes me, fully takes me, don't wait. If you do, he'll be impossible to stop."

She looks over her shoulder, staring into my eyes. We have

an understanding. She won't wait.

We walk in silence for thirty minutes before coming to the end of our side tunnel. It exits into a larger tunnel where a river flows down, all the way to the massive chamber Behemoth calls home, where the gates of Tartarus await.

As Em starts for the tunnel, I'm suddenly glad I decided to breathe through my nose. A new odor has entered the mix, and it's hard to separate from the others at first, but once I do, I lunge for Em and snatch her arm, stopping her just a few feet from the small tunnel's exit. When she looks back at me, I put my index finger to my lip and shush her.

She mouths, "What is it?"

I put my hand atop my head, bending in a way that is instantly recognizable to any hunter as a cresty. Her eyes go wide. She closes her mouth and takes a few quick sniffs through her nose. She winces at the smell, but fights through it until she detects them too.

Somehow knowing it's been detected, a large cresty lowers its head into the tunnel. It was waiting just outside, ready to snatch up whoever walked out of the tunnel next!

Or was it?

This cresty is acting strangely, just staring at us. The scent of a hunter is enough to trigger a strong fight or flight response in cresties. They either turn tail and run, or hiss and prepare for a fight. This one does neither. It simply looks at us.

Not us, I realize. *At me.*

I take a step forward.

It takes a step back.

I repeat the action, and the cresty does as well.

It's giving me a wide berth.

Does it recognize me? Is it— "Grumpy?"

I walk toward the creature, reaching out an open palm. The cresty lowers its head.

"Solomon!" Emilie hisses. "Get back here!"

I ignore her and continue out into the large tunnel, entering the river until I'm knee deep and my hand is just a foot from the dinosaur's snout. "It is you," I say, "isn't it?"

The twenty foot cresty male takes a single step forward, placing its forehead gently under my hand. Emilie's telltale gasp issues from the tunnel behind me and Grumpy lifts his head and looks at Em.

I turn my back to Grumpy, which once again makes Em gasp, but I trust this creature. I don't know if it's because the cresties are so old, predating the Nephilim occupation of Antarctica, that I am in some ways bonded to them as I am to the land, or if it's merely the fact that I killed Alice and the intelligent dinosaurs feel some kind of obligation, but the connection is real.

Em holds two knives at the ready. They seem like tiny weapons to use against a large carnivore, but she'd have no trouble blinding the creature and then moving in closer for the kill, which is something I really don't want her to do.

"Em, put the knives away," I say.

She hesitates.

"Em, he's a friend."

She looks at me, then to Grumpy, then back to me. Finally, she sheaths the knives.

"Come here," I say.

Her hands stay near the knives, but she comes forward slowly. "He's not alone," she whispers, watching the tunnel around us.

"I know," I reply. "There are eleven others."

"You can smell each one?"

"No," I say with a grin. "We're old friends."

She stops a few feet away.

I stand aside. "Em this is Grumpy. Grumpy, Em."

The two size each other up. When Grumpy takes a step forward, Em flinches and reaches for a knife. I stop her with a stern, "Em."

She holds her ground, but can't erase the fear from her face. If Grumpy sneezes she's libel to slit his throat.

"Hold out your hand," I say.

She does, and Grumpy sniffs her hand. When her hand comes in contact with the cresty's snout, Em smiles. "I've never touched a live one before." Grumpy slides his head beneath her hand and she rubs him. The big dinosaur lets out a deep rumble, like a giant cat purring. "How is this possible?" Em asks.

"I set them free," I say. "When I saved Kainda from Alice. She dominated the pack at the time." I rub Grumpy's neck. "How did you get free? Was there an exit I didn't find?" I ask, but the dinosaur can't speak. "And why are you here?"

When Grumpy turns toward me, I get a sense of why he's here. To repay the favor. To help me fight. To be my army. How that's possible, I have no idea. But I think that's what's going on.

"Do you have anything of Luca's?" I ask Em.

She nods and digs into one of her pouches. She takes out a crayon and small wad of folded pages. "I thought they would help him feel safe."

I take the crayon and paper and hold them out to Grumpy's nose. He smells them. "Leave him unharmed," I say, and then hand the drawing supplies back to Em. "He knows our scents now. Hopefully he understands."

"Hopefully?"

"I think he does."

Grumpy lifts his head and lets out a high pitched bark. Eleven more cresties, ranging in size from ten to eighteen feet, step out from the shadows. The whole deadly gang is here. Grumpy turns to face me again. I give his nose a pat. And then the lot of them is off and running, disappearing into the darkness. I wish there were a way to communicate with the beasts, to forge some kind of official plan, but I get the sense that Grumpy understands their role in the events to come.

At least, I think he does.

31

As we approach the end of our journey, we stop to share a last meal. We sit by the river, lit by a large number of glowing crystals embedded in the wall, and eat the fruits of our recent hunt. The centipede is hardly appetizing, but its cheesy flesh is high in protein and will help combat fatigue from our journey. I'm going to need all the strength I can muster soon enough. We scoop the uncooked flesh out with our hands and scrape it onto our lower teeth before swallowing. I notice Emilie having a hard time swallowing.

She sees me watching and says, "It's been a long time since I ate centipede."

I take a big bite and force myself to casually swallow without showing the disgust I feel. "It's an acquired taste."

We both laugh through mouthfuls of centipaste.

"What's it like?" Em asks me. "The outside world? Do things taste better there?"

My mind flashes through a thousand different flavors. Chocolate ice cream. Maria's Pizza. Roast beef. Devil Dogs. Corn on the cob. Despite the disgusting flavor in my mouth, and worse smell in the air, my mouth starts to water. "Like you wouldn't believe."

"Do you think…"

"I don't know," I say, anticipating her question. I want to tell her she can trust me to succeed. That I can face the devil, return and take her to the outside world, live with my parents and eat candy until we puke. But I'm not even sure I believe that's possible.

"What about everything else? Is it…safe?"

"Most of the time," I say, but then remember scores of news reports about wars and famines. "Where I'm from. But not everywhere. Some places aren't much different than here. And there have been wars—" I shake my head. The images of war retained in my head aren't doing my nerves any good.

She nods like she knows what I'm talking about. "It's what they've been working towards. People killing people. Only things haven't worked out the way they want. Which is why they need you. To speed things up. Set mankind against each other."

At first I have no idea what she's talking about, but then I slowly put the pieces together. There are Nephilim in the world. I don't know where or how, or what they look like, but they're out there. And if what she's saying is true, then they've been influencing the outside world for a long time. Causing wars. Building tension. Hoping humans will pull the trigger on themselves. And while wars have raged and millions died, humanity is still here and more populous and powerful than ever.

But how can I change that? Even instilled with the spirit of Nephil, I'm still just one person. I might be able to control the earth, air and water here on Antarctica, but that won't help with the rest of the world, and those powers might fade when I leave. Could Nephil be that strong of a leader that the giant Nephilim are afraid to proceed without him? Perhaps his presence will erase tension between the different classes and unite them against the surface world? All of this is possible, but none of it feels right. There's something else at work. Unfortunately, the only way to figure out what that is, is to take on the mantel of Ull and offer myself—willingly—to Nephil. And by then, it might be too late to change anything.

I've lost my appetite and fling a fist full of centipaste on the cave floor. "We should go," I say. "Before I change my mind."

Em swallows her last bite with an, "Ugh," and begins to pack up.

I squat by the river, washing my hands. I see my face, lit by the glow of the crystals, reflected in the smoothly flowing water. I inspect my hair. It's still red with Em's blood. But then I see my face, and for the first time I notice how different I look. My jaw is square and when I bite down the sides of my face bulge with muscle. But even stranger than that is my skin. It looks fuzzy. I put my hand to my face and rub. I'm covered in coarse red fuzz. I realize what it is at the same time Emilie speaks about it.

"Leave your beard alone," she says, and then notices my stunned face. She draws two knives. "What is it?"

"I have a beard?"

She puts the knives away and squats next to me. "You're of age."

"Why didn't you say anything?"

"Why would I? You've always had it."

That I've now had a beard for months, maybe longer, without realizing it stuns me. "Why didn't Aimee say anything about it?"

She shrugs. "She had other things to say." She spins a knife between two fingers. "Do you want me to cut it off?"

I look at myself again. The hair makes me look older. Stronger. Like a man. "No," I say. "Leave it. Ull would like it."

I stand and take the cresty hood and cloak out of a large satchel. I shake out the cloak and wrap it around my shoulders.

"What would Grumpy think of that?" Em asks.

"Depends," I say.

"On what?"

"If they were friends."

Em gets out a final laugh. And then we're down to business. We pack out what's left of our gear, I position the skull hood atop my head and we set out for the great cavern.

We reach our destination quickly and stop where the river divides and criss-crosses into the distance. Maybe a half mile to our right is a line of fire rising ten feet tall. Through its flickering flames I see hunters and smaller Nephilim. Standing high above the flames are Nephilim warriors facing our direction. They're not looking at us, though, they're looking beyond us. I follow their gaze and find the subject of their attention.

Behemoth.

The giant is squatting, but still looks like a living skyscraper. Its body heaves with each breath and I realize that the wind in this cavern might be partly generated by the thing's breathing. Tendrils of its rope-like hair twitch like the tails of angry cats. Behemoth is ready to pounce, but maintains his distance.

Em sees the confusion on my face and says, "The flames keep him at bay. Not because of the heat, but the light."

"Ahh," I say. Behemoth lives in total and perpetual darkness. There are no crystals here. No natural sources of light. This doesn't stop the giant from seeing—it's adjusted to pitch black just like the rest of us—but it does make the creature sensitive to light. The thing is probably tortured by the bright glow of the flames even at this distance. The question is, can it be agitated enough that it will ignore the flames? After all, Ull *should* make a grand entrance.

I turn to Emilie. "So, this is it."

Sadness creeps into her face. "Will I see you again?"

When I don't reply, she adds, "You can lie to me."

I grin. "Then yes. But don't focus on me. Look for Doug first. See if he recovered Luca. If he did, take him and don't look back. If he failed and they still have him, wait for a distraction, and then strike."

"What distraction?"

"I'll think of something," I say. "But when the time comes. Don't hesitate. Strike. Luca won't be a priority once I'm there, so you shouldn't have to deal with Ninnis or Kainda."

Her eyes darken at the mention of Ninnis.

"We're not here for vengeance," I say. "Just Luca."

"And if we recover him and escape," she asks. "What then?"

It blows my mind that we haven't talked about this before.

We've been so focused on getting Luca back that we never came up with what to do after we had him. "We'll take you both to McMurdo. You can take Luca and live on the outside, eat delicious food, and maybe find your family."

"How?" She asks. "Will you be coming?"

I shake my head, no, but I suspect she knew that. "I need to stay here. When they find you, tell them you belong to Merrill Clark in Portsmouth, New Hampshire, United States of America. When they bring you to him, tell him the truth. Tell him about me. He will help you."

Loud chanting from Behemoth's cavern snaps our heads toward the wall of fire. Time is short. "It's time," I say.

Em lunges forward and wraps her arms around me. Her embrace is crushing, but fuels my resolve and reminds me of why I'm facing my fears today instead of running away. Without another word, we part and walk in opposite directions, Em disappearing into the dark tunnel and me walking into the brightly lit cavern in full view of the Nephilim—and Behemoth.

32

My heart beats in time with my footsteps, each booming with the intensity of thunder. At least, that's how it feels to me. Because the moment I'm out in the open, two things happen. First, the Nephilim chanting stops as though someone has taken the needle off a record. I feel thousands of eyes upon me, though I cannot see them. The Nephilim and hunters are concealed behind a wall of flame and radiating heat that I cannot feel, but can see shimmering up toward the ceiling hundreds of feet above.

Second, Behemoth holds its breath. I don't see it happen, but the breeze has died down and the pressure of the place has changed. It's amazing that a single creature could have that much influence on its environment. It's also terrifying.

Everything about this is terrifying. I'm no longer Ull. I'm not facing my enemies with the confidence of a warrior who would fight to the death. I'm the nerdy bookworm and despite having gained some skills, abilities, and admittedly, some toughening up, my idea of a good fight is still a rousing game of Risk or Electronic

Battleship.

But I'm pretending to be Ull, so I keep my chin up, my eyes set forward and my stride confident. I hide my fear and press onward, for Luca.

When I reach the center of the chamber, still a few hundred feet from the fire, the ground shakes. My presence on this side of the flame has spurred Behemoth into action, as I feared, and hoped, it would.

I don't look back.

I don't quicken my pace.

For those looking at my face, it will appear as though I am as unconcerned by Behemoth's approach as I would be by an ant's.

A second quake rattles the cavern, this one more intense, but still not on top of me. My body flickers from the orange flames. If I could feel heat, I suspect I would be quite warm now.

Boom.

Behemoth takes another giant step. It's right behind me now. Close enough.

Without moving my hands or changing my facial expression, I focus on the air at the top of the cavern. I turn my focus smaller and smaller, separating one gas from another until I've found what I'm looking for: oxygen.

I can hear Behemoth's hairy tendrils snaking toward me. It won't be long before they strike out, lash around me and drag me back to the giant jaws sporting teeth the size of sailboat sails. If that were to happen, I'm not sure I could set myself free, even with all of my abilities.

When I'm sure my fear is about to reveal itself on my face, I bring the cloud of oxygen down to the fire. The reaction is instantaneous. The flames burst white hot, filling the cavern with a sudden burst of light akin to a giant sized camera flash bulb. I close my eyes are the same moment, sparing myself from the majority of the light's power.

Behemoth roars behind me. The sound is so loud that it takes all my strength to not put my hands to my ears.

As the flames shrink back to normal size, I realize that I could do the chicken dance all the way up to the flame wall and no one would notice. The bright light and intense sound have had an effect on the Nephilim too. Several rub their eyes. Some rub their ears. But not one of them is watching me now.

I don't waver. Just because everyone I can see isn't paying attention, doesn't mean others aren't still watching. I continue toward the fire, my pace as even as it was when I first entered the chamber.

The first hunters and Nephilim to regain their sight see me as I approach the flames. A murmur rises up. They no doubt expected me to arrive on their side of the fire wall and avoid Behemoth altogether. I can't hear what's being said, but they're probably wondering if I've gone mad.

So I prepare to continue the show. But before I use my ability to split the wall of fire in two and walk through, I have a revelation. Not only can I not feel cold, but it has no effect on my body. I don't get frostbite or hypothermia. No matter how cold things get, or how strong the wind blows, I am immune to the cold. And I think the same holds true for heat. So instead of parting the fire before me, I step right in.

A grin spreads onto my face as the orange flames lick pain-lessly around me. But I notice my clothing and belongings catch fire and I quickly create a protective vortex of wind around my body. Ull might not mind stepping out of the fire buck naked, but I don't think I could hide my embarrassment.

Once free of the flames, I realize I'm still grinning. But Ull would do the same, so I keep the smile and meet the eyes of every hunter and Nephilim waiting for me. I see many I recognize from experience and by their garb and headdresses. Thor, son of Odin, Norse god of thunder and Kainda's master, wielding his hammer and wearing a great horned helmet. The Egyptian Horus, god of vengeance, wearing a helmet shaped like a falcon and carrying a two pronged spear. Next comes Hades, brother of Zeus, whom I identify by the pet he holds by a chain: Cerberus, a three headed creature with the body of a giant red-furred wolf, its three heads resembling feeders—black orb eyes and triangle teeth. It's a hor-rid thing and I fight not to show my revulsion.

When the first Nephilim drops to one knee and bows, this becomes easier, in part because they can't see me, but also because my show has worked and it's quite possible that *they* fear *me*. They weren't entirely sure what would happen when I bonded with the body of Nephil, and they most likely assume I've taken on some supernatural abilities.

The sea of Nephilim and hunters separates, offering me a path that stretches like a freeway through their ranks for four hundred feet. I see more familiar Nephilim including the obese Gaia, whose beaked face and rolls of feather covered fat make my stomach twist with disgust, not only from her grotesque appearance, but also at the knowledge that the feeders I ate in the pit emerged from her girth. As did the duplicate of my mother.

It occurs to me that Gaia knows the truth about me. That I needed to be broken once again. How many others know? Kainda for sure. Ninnis trusted her with the knowledge, which means there is a bond of father and daughter between them that neither would ever admit. I look at Gaia and see a glimmer of fear in her eyes. But she's not afraid of Ull, I realize. She's afraid of the truth being revealed. Of me not pulling off this monumental bluff. If I'm not Ull, it means not only Ninnis failed, but so did Gaia, as the breeder overseeing my rebreaking. The punishment for failure would no doubt be severe. The punishment for this deception? Well, that might very well mean a trip through the giant gates I now see before me.

The gates stand fifty feet tall and half as wide. They're black, and metal, I think. I expected ornate decorations, perhaps an inscription or some kind of gilding, but the two doors are simply as black as night. In fact, the bright fire light doesn't show on the doors. It's like they're actually *absorbing* the light.

But the strange doors don't hold my attention for long. Enki stands before me, dressed in his black leathers. And Ninnis stands by his side, though his near six foot height takes him only up to a level slightly below the giant's knee. He stares at me with an intensity that matches the wall of fire, probably wondering if I will play his game.

When I see Luca off to the side, and Kainda next to him, there is no doubt that I will play my part to the very end. Behind them stands a pair of young hunters, one male, one female, who I assume are Preeg and Pyke. I glance around them, finding no sign of Doug.

As I approach, Enki drops to one knee and bows. Ninnis, Kainda and the others follow suit. When their eyes are downcast, I turn my eyes to Luca. He looks frightened, but manages to show a slight grin when I wink at him. The wink tells him that not only am I here, but I'm also me. Not Ull. But if he's seen any of my recent experiences, he might already know that.

The sound of standing bodies brings my eyes forward again, and then up. Enki looks down at me with a toothy grin that looks more savage than happy.

"I was not sure you would come after so long," the giant says, his voice like the roar of an eighteen wheeler.

"The effect of bonding with the body of Nephil was…profound," I say, fighting the quiver in my voice. "It took some time to adjust."

"I should say so," Enki says. "But your return has fortuitous timing. Human technology is progressing faster than ever and the time to strike, and undo their advantage, is upon us."

Something about the things he is saying confuses me, so I offer a cocky laugh and ask, "How far could they have advanced in two years that *we* would have anything to fear from *them*?"

Enki's grin spreads as he lets out a deep chuckle. Even Ninnis is smiling. My anger rises. I *hate* being out of the loop, especially when people—even Nephilim—laugh at me.

"How long has it been?" I ask.

The laughing continues and starts to spread beyond our small group. I put my hand on Whipsnap, add a snarl to my voice and ask again. "How. Long."

Laughter fades. Smiles falter. Ull is angry.

"In surface years?" Enki asks.

"Yes," I say.

"Twenty years."

33

I nearly throw up on Enki's oversized feet. The news hits me hard and deep. I feel like I'm facing the feeder duplicate of my mother all over again—a perversion of reality. How could twenty surface years have passed? It's just not possible. Sure, I've got some facial hair growing, but I have a hairy father and a fifteen year old needing to shave is actually quite common. But what felt like two years to me was actually *twenty*?

The ramifications of this news slam into my thoughts like tidal waves.

My parents are in their sixties. Maybe dead. They've long since given up any hope of finding me alive and might have other kids. They've moved on. Forgotten me.

Justin isn't a kid any more. He might be married. He might have kids of his own. A family.

Dr. Clark will have given up on me as well. He's an old man by now. In his sixties if he's still alive. Maybe remarried. Twenty years without a wife is a long time.

My heart aches when I think of Mira. The girl that I held so close to my heart for so long is no longer a girl. She's a woman. And like Justin, she might have a family. A husband. The thought fills me with jealousy and anger.

"You seem surprised," Ninnis says, returning my thoughts to the awful here and now.

"I'm thirty-three years old?" I say.

"According to the outside world, yes. Give or take a few years," Ninnis says. "It's not an exact science." He looks me over. "You must have been deep. Time slows the deeper you go. You don't look much older than you did when we last saw you."

I feel my legs growing weak. My head spins. Everything has changed. Everything I hoped to get back has been taken from me. While I didn't had my family, friends or life before, the knowledge that geography was the only thing that separated us comforted me. Crossing the ocean, or catching a plane flight from McMurdo, wasn't an impossibility. But the distance between me and everything I knew before is now separated by an insurmountable divide—time.

I glance at Luca and see concern in his eyes. My resolve is wavering and it shows on my face. Looking into his eyes reminds me that I'm not here for me. I'm here for him. I erase the surprise from my face and straighten my back. "Well then, we shouldn't waste any more time."

Ninnis squints at me, never taking his eyes away from mine. "Agreed."

Enki steps to the side, revealing a thirty foot circle carved into the stone floor in front of the giant gates. Within the circle are an array of symbols, some of them familiar, some of them new, but all fill me with a sense of dread. I'm facing an ancient evil. Something still so far beyond my understanding. But I sense these symbols hold power, and when I see the smaller circle dead center in the middle of the larger, I know that is where I am meant to stand.

"The ceremony requires a sacrifice of human blood," Ninnis says.

I worry that he will choose to use Luca, but his next words erase that fear.

"To expedite things, we took care of that before you arrived." Ninnis reaches behind his back, pulls something from a satchel and tosses it towards me.

As the object spins through the air, I catch glimpses of red hair and a face. It's a head. He's just thrown a human head at me. As the head lands and rolls to a stop at my feet, I think, *don't react, don't react, don't react!* And that proves incredibly hard to do when I see the blank eyes of Doug staring up at me from my feet. I swallow hard and ask, "He was a hunter?"

"A volunteer," Ninnis says.

When I look up at him, I see anger in his eyes. Ninnis knew I sent Doug to take Luca. And Doug clearly failed in the attempt.

"He willingly died for you," Ninnis adds, turning the knife.

"As you all would," I say to Ninnis.

I'm as surprised by the statement as Ninnis is, but he has no choice but to nod and agree.

"Little Ull," Enki says with a chuckle. "You have not changed."

I look up at the giant, at the gold band around his forehead
that hides the Nephilim's weak spot. I could knock the crown
from his head and impale him with Whipsnap before he even
knew what was happening. I blink the thought from my mind.
Either my proximity to the gates, or maybe all these Nephilim,
are triggering my dark imagination, a problem that has not pla-
gued me since the personalities of Ull and Nephil were locked
away inside my mind. "I am stronger," I say.

"Of that, I have no doubt," Enki said. "There is a resolve in
your eyes that was not there before."

I nod. "I am ready."

Enki sweeps his huge hand out toward the circle. "Take your
place at the center. The ceremony will be a rebirth for you, violent and painful. But it will also be brief."

I head into the circle, feeling sick to my stomach as I step
past the outer ring of symbols. I stop in the center and turn
around.

"When we next speak, you will be Nephil, Lord of the Nephilim and commander of all that you see!" Enki opens his arms
out to either side. I think that if I curled up in a ball my whole
body could fit inside his bicep. "The army of Nephil will rise
again."

I scan the thousands of hunters and Nephilim standing
around me. The heroes of old. The men of renown. I can't imagine a modern army that could stand against such a force. How
the ancient humans forced the Nephilim underground, I have no
idea. But there is no time for such pondering. I search the sea of
hunters to my right, looking for a familiar face. Finding none, I

turn to the left, putting on a phony smile as I do. I see Luca there. Kainda is by his side. Preeg and Pyke maintain their vigil behind them. But I don't see what I'm—

There! In the shadows of the far wall behind Preeg and Pyke. A subtle shift in the darkness. Emilie is there. Waiting to strike. One girl against an army.

But there is another I'm searching for. My only real hope of escaping this situation with my life and my soul intact. I don't see him with my eyes so I reach out to him with my mind.

Xin, I think. *Can you hear me?*

Are you near, brother?

I need you, Xin.

Xin!

My silence has stretched on too long. It has become awkward. They are waiting for a response from me.

So I give them one.

I turn my head to the ceiling and let out a howl. It's only a moment before the others join in. Thousands of human and Nephilim heads turn toward the ceiling and roar. The ground shakes beneath my feet. When Behemoth—who is also a Nephilim—joins in, bits and pieces of the ceiling shake loose and fall.

When the mass howl completes, I feel more afraid than ever. When Ull was a part of me, the howl filled me with energy and confidence. Now, I feel drained by it. But I stand my ground in the circle, and wait for what comes next.

Six Nephilim step forward. I recognize each one of them from history books and carvings all around the underworld. Enki. His brother, Enlil. The sons of Nephil. Odin. Osiris. Zeus. The last is a new face to me, but I think he's Marduk, king of the early Mesopotamian gods. These are the ancient kings of this world, who once ruled over humanity. They radiate power and sinister intentions. They stand around the circle, chanting in Sumerian.

Enki stretches out his arms. The others follow suit. Their finger tips touch, forming a circle of Nephilim flesh around me. He speaks in Sumerian and Thor steps out of the crowd wielding his hammer and carrying a large satchel. He stops behind Enki and removes a nail so large that it looks more like a thick sword. He places the nail against the back of Enki's six fingered hand. And with a single solid whack from Mjöllnir, sends the nail through.

Enki twitches from the impact, but shows no pain. Instead, his face reflects delight. His smile grows wider still when Thor puts a giant nail through his other hand and then moves on to Enlil. One by one, Thor slams the nails through the hands of the ancient kings. With the nails still in their flesh, the wounds cannot heal and their dark purple blood drains onto the floor. The carved out ring fills with the blood of the six warriors. It rolls from the outer circle and into the array of symbols.

My eyes widen as I see the rivers of blood snake across the floor. I follow the path forward and realize that it will soon fill the circle around me and drain into the slightly depressed area in which I stand. I will soon be standing in a pool of their blood, which when diluted can heal a human, but at full strength can kill. I'm either meant to die in their blood and be reborn with the spirit of Nephil, or it's meant to heal me from the severe injury caused by the bonding. Neither option is appealing.

As I watch the blood slither toward me, I nearly miss the whisper in my ear.

Solomon.

Not in my ear. In my head.

Solomon.

Xin?

Yes.

Can you help me?

You reached out to me, he says. *How?*

I don't know.

Then answer this, why did you call me 'brother'?

34

Do you know about the experiments? I think to Xin. *The duplicates of me?*

Abominations, he replies. *Destroyed as they should have been.*

Not all of them.

How do you know? Xin asks.

A teacher, I think, but I keep Aimee's identity hidden. *She told me some were left alive. Six of them.*

The blood of six Nephilim races around the carved out tracks that end in six straight lines. The lines lead to the circle surrounding me. It won't be long.

Impossible, Xin says.

I'm not sure where Xin is. It's possible he's not even in the chamber, but I ask, *Can you see the boy with Kainda?*

I can.

Search his face. His eyes. They are mine.

Xin says nothing for a moment.

During his silence, the six trails of blood reach the inner circle simultaneously and begin to surround me.

Search his mind if you have to!

More silence. The blood is close to spilling over into the shallow bowl in which I stand.

It's true, Xin says. *He is you.*

Not me, I think. *My brother.*

Xin is intelligent. Like me. So I know he's understood what I'm telling him. But I say it clearly for him so there is no chance of a misunderstanding. *You are my brother, Xin. As is Luca, the boy. You were both created...from me. We are family. We are brothers.*

Xin doesn't reply and I fear the silence will be permanent this time. Xin, in many ways, is a monster. He is half Nephilim, after all, born from a breeder, unlike Luca, whose mother was human. But Xin is also good. He showed that to me when he saved my life. I believe he sensed the bond between us even then. But I fear the revelation of his true origin might be more than he can process.

I reach out to him one more time, *Xin! Speak to me!* But he does not return and even he if did, I would not hear him. The blood circle overflows. Trickling paths of blood slip over the side and roll toward my feet. As it does, Enki shouts a command.

Chains snap taut and fifty Nephilim giants grunt as they put all their strength into pulling open the gates of Tartarus. Enki turns his face toward me. "Ull, chosen of the Nephilim, do you willingly give yourself to the spirit of Nephil?"

My breath quickens as my heart pumps adrenaline through my veins. I glance to Luca. He looks as terrified as me. My eyes shift to Kainda. She's watching me with an expression that catches me off guard.

There is pity in her eyes.

She knows I am not Ull. She knows what I am sacrificing for the boy.

Her eyes glisten and a single tear falls.

I look back up at Enki. "I do."

The blood reaches my feet.

A searing heat reaches up through my body, burning like the sun. I scream, but remain rooted in place. My body convulses. I feel my mind and thoughts fading, but I fight for lucidity.

There is chanting all around me now, loud and insistent.

A strong wind billows past me, but it has nothing to do with my abilities. Until Luca is safe, I cannot reveal myself. A loud groan like a fog horn rolls out of the opening doors. Through blurry vision, I see only blackness beyond the doors. But somewhere in the dark, something moves.

I hear the name of Nephil repeated again and again as the chanting grows more fervent. And then I see it. A black shape, like a cloud, reaching out for me, stretching its limbs out like a striking squid.

The black tendrils reach me and stab into my chest, clutching my chest in a frigid grip. I feel my heart stop, but the heat burning up from my feet restarts it. I die again and again, but am quickly brought back each time.

Pain explodes in my stomach and then surges through my body as though it's flowing through my veins. I'm not sure if I've stopped screaming yet, but I'm suddenly aware of my shrieking voice again. The pain moves up through my chest. My jugular feels like it will burst as the pain moves higher. And then it's in my head. There is a flash of white hot pain and then the world ceases to exist.

The circle of blood is gone.

The army of Nephilim is no more.

The cavern. Behemoth. Luca. Kainda. All gone.

I am alone in a world of painless white.

A voice booms around me. "Who are you?"

"Solomon Ull Vincent," I say.

"The chosen?"

"I am," I say.

"Why have you locked me away?"

This is Nephil, I realize. And he knows I've locked away the small bit of his personality that was transferred to me when I consumed his flesh.

"Because," I say, flexing my hands and gritting my teeth. "This is my body. My mind. And it will never belong to you!"

"You think you can resist me?" The voice shouts and suddenly I'm standing in front of the mental vault door Xin helped put in place. The black form is there too, flowing with black tendrils. It reaches for the door, snakes its way into the cracks and pulls.

The door shatters into pieces.

In that instant I lose myself. Nephil is supercharged as the darkness within the vault merges with his spirit. I feel myself reaching out, beyond my physical body, out into the continent. Antarctica becomes an extension of me like never before. I can feel its mass as though it were my own body. Its rivers are my blood. The snow, my skin.

But my reach doesn't end there.

I feel the ocean beyond.

And more land. South America first. Australia. North America. Europe. Asia. I feel the tectonic plates, shifting and grinding above the molten layer beneath. For one explosive moment I feel bound to the entire planet. But I'm out of control, or rather, under control. I grip the entire planet, holding it, holding myself...and spin. I feel my skin come loose and wrap around my body, tearing and grinding, exploding and burning.

I scream, falling to my knees and clutching my head. The connection is broken. The darkness swirls before me. Nephil is reborn and whole again, inside my body. Inside my mind. And I stand against him, alone.

"Not alone, Solomon" a voice replies to my thoughts. It's my voice, but deeper and more confident. Ull emerges from the broken vault.

"You're stronger than the last time we met," he says.

"And you're not trying to kill me. Don't you want to be bonded with Nephil?" I ask.

"I spent enough time with the beast to know he has no intention of sharing our body with me. He seeks to destroy us. To make our body his own. This cannot happen." He suddenly has Whipsnap in his hand. "We must fight him together. As one."

Laughter shakes the world apart. We are surrounded by the dark, standing in a pillar of light. I find a duplicate of Whipsnap in my hands and I stand back to back with Ull.

The darkness sweeps around us. I see eyes. Yellow eyes. And

claws. Razor sharp. We stand in the eye of an evil hurricane, but the wind is laughter—mocking, hateful laughter.

"Stand your ground, Solomon," Ull says. "This is our mind. You bound him once, you can do it again."

The laughter reaches a high pitch as a streak of black separates and swoops toward me. Blazing yellow eyes burn at me. Claws reach out. I swing Whipsnap down, bringing the blade into and through the thing's torso. I strike nothing. The blade has passed through the body as though it is immaterial. The thing's claws, however, are solid.

Four red streaks appear on my side. A blazing pain follows. I smell my blood and feel its warmth on my side. I look down. The gash is deep. Fearing my organs will slip out, I drop Whipsnap and press my hands against the wound.

Ull shouts a battle cry and swings. He screams in pain, but swings again, and again.

We fall to our knees together. Defeated.

As the dark swirling hatred moves in to consume us, I say, "I forgive you, Ull."

He looks over his shoulder and meets my eyes. His face is covered in blood. "Too late."

I nod. My separate sides, unable to reconcile, are weaker on their own. I cannot stand up to the monster. I don't even stand a chance. I lower my head in defeat.

"Get up," a raspy voice says.

"You aren't alone," says a second, younger voice.

I look up to find Xin and Luca standing above Ull and me.

Xin reaches his hand down to me. "It's time to fight, brother."

35

Xin pulls me up and I see little Luca yank Ull to his feet. The boy is stronger than anyone would believe.

Xin's yellow eyes are just inches from mine. "Remember," he says. "This is your mind. Your rules. To win, you will need to believe that. We can support you, but the fight is yours."

I look at Ull. "What about him?"

"Ull is your heart," Xin says. He gives you strength, but this fight is taking place in your mind. And that is *your* domain."

I'm not sure what surprises me more, that Xin is here with Luca or that Ull has been identified as my heart. But I suppose it makes sense. He is all passion and fire, while I am logical and thoughtful. It doesn't mean I'm without heart. It just means that Ull is the part of me that feels the deepest, and since the breaking that part of me has been angry. Full of rage. Destructive.

The blackness known as Nephil has shifted away from the four of us, perhaps contemplating this new development.

"Heal your wounds," Xin says.

I look down and tell myself that this isn't real. That it's all in my mind. And that my wounds are imaginary. The gashes seal and the blood flow stops. The pain, however, doesn't fade.

Ull seems to fare better. Not only are his wounds gone, but he looks like he could take on a polar bear in a wrestling match and come out unscathed. I suppose it's easy to let go of reality when you're all heart. My mind has a hard time accepting that this reality, isn't real. But I do my best, because I suspect all the physical strength in the world will matter little in this place.

The darkness howls and spins closer. The four of us form a circle. Ull is to my back, Xin to my right and Luca to my left. Each one of us now holds a Whipsnap of our own. "Stand your ground!" I shout.

The specters swarm again, their yellow eyes burning. They attack, one at a time, swooping, striking. I feel their claws pass through me, but remind myself that they cannot hurt my body, because it doesn't exist here.

But the effort is tiring. I sense the others losing strength, too. And as we tire, Nephil grows stronger.

Ull shouts, swinging Whipsnap at everything that comes close, but to no effect.

"Ull," I shout over the howling wind. "Do you feel it?"

"What are you talking about?" He shouts back.

"This wind. In your hair. Between your fingers. It belongs to us."

He turns to me and I see the blackness assault his back. He grits his teeth and gives it no attention. I face him and put out my hands.

"We will settle things between us," he says. "When this is over."

I nod, and he puts his hands in mine. A blast of emotion fills my mind. All of Ull's anger is passed on. All of his power. And something surprising: love. But there is no time to dwell on this. I siphon his energy, my energy, and build a cyclone of my own. It radiates out from us, enveloping Luca and Xin and shielding all of us from further attack.

Xin turns to me, shouting over the rushing wind. "You cannot contain him this time! He is too strong!"

"Then what?" I ask.

"You must expel him!" Xin shouts. "Cast him out! Without a body, he will be undone."

So I push.

And my cyclone expands against the darkness. I feel myself growing weary, the drain of using the elements seems to affect me even in my mind. But still, I push harder. Ull screams, his rage fueling me.

"You're doing it, Sol!" Luca shouts. The boy's voice and the innocence I hear in it strengthens my resolve.

My scream merges with Ull's, our combined voice exploding the whirlwind outward. The blackness bursts. The white world returns.

Ull and I both fall to our knees, heaving with each breath.

"Did…it work?" I ask.

"Almost," Xin says. "He is wounded, but still here."

I look up and see the darkness retreating into the form of a Nephilim warrior. The black giant staggers back as though struck, clutching his stomach. When the thing lifts up its head, yellow eyes glow at us.

"Get up, brothers," Xin says, his voice filled with urgency. "We cannot let him regroup!"

Before I can get up, Xin charges with a battle cry. To my surprise, Luca follows him, Whipsnap raised to strike.

Ull looks over at me. I can see his blazing eyes and savage grin behind the curtain of red hair that hangs over his face. "Come, Sol," he says. "Let's finish this."

We rise together, running side by side. The wind at our backs lifts us into the air, our twin Whipsnaps poised to strike.

Xin reaches Nephil first and slices a deep cut into the thing's leg. But it does no damage and he's kicked aside. Luca fares no better as he strikes and passes right through the leg. He stumbles and falls behind the giant. Ull and I share a glance as we descend toward Nephil. We're thinking the same thing.

Of course we are, I think. *We are me.*

Ull arrives first, stabbing Whipsnap at the giant's chest. But the action is a ruse. He spins the weapon around, bringing the mace side up toward Nephil's head. At the same moment, I put my mind to work, imagining the golden ring that protects the Nephilim soft spot.

There is a clang of metal on metal and the ring is knocked free. And where the ring once was, there is now flesh. Not blackness. Not some supernatural cloud. The forehead revealed beneath the ring undulates with a pulse.

With a battle cry that would make Ull proud, I draw Whipsnap back, take aim and thrust it forward. The tip strikes flesh and tears through.

A scream more horrible than anything I've heard—the scream of a being that has waited thousands of years to be set free from a prison or torment—tears through my mind.

And then I'm back. In the real world.

There is no longer blood at my feet. Instead it covers the bodies and faces of the six Nephilim kings still standing around me. The cyclone I created in my mind must have been formed here as well. When exhaustion pulls me to my knees, I have no doubt.

I realize that the massive chamber has fallen silent. I scan the faces around me. They're not looking at me, they're looking above me. I turn my head up and find the blackness of Nephil spinning above my head.

That's when a terrible pain clutches my body. I curl in upon myself as something burrows through me. My stomach sours and feels heavy. After three hard contractions, I pitch forward and heave. I feel a thickness rising in my throat. I heave again and feel it stick. I cannot breathe! With the last of my strength and breath, I heave one last time. When the thing comes loose and spills from my mouth, I scream and then suck in a loud breath.

I feel the room's attention turn back to me. And then to the object lying in front of me.

It's a thick, dark, purple blob, like a large, bloody loogie.

The body of Nephil.

36

I stare at the viscous blob that sat undigested in my stomach for so many years. It's a horrible, sinister thing. And though it is immobile, the body of Nephil is alive with hatred. I can feel it, even now, reaching out for me.

That's when I realize what has happened here. The spirit of Nephil hovers above me. But it has not tried to possess me again. Because it can't! Not without a part of its body in the host. I am free! The elation that Tobias felt upon hearing the news of Ull's demise must have felt something like this.

But that's not all. The potential to strike a devastating blow against the Nephilim sits before me, wiggling like Jello-O. If I destroy the body of Nephil, his spirit will not be able to join with a body—mine or anyone else's—and if he does not do that soon, he will cease to exist.

Fighting exhaustion, I yank Whipsnap from my belt, spin the weapon above my head, and prepare to crush the glob of ancient blood beneath the mace. I begin my downward swing. Whipsnap's shaft bends from the motion and when it springs forward will add its own energy to the blow.

I vaguely register a screaming voice. "No!"

An arm appears between Whipsnap's mace and the glob of blood. The weapon strikes hard and a loud crack sounds out as the bones within the arm snap. A scream of pain follows and I reel away from it.

Ninnis stands before me, his left forearm bent at a sick angle. The body of Nephil remains on the floor, unharmed. The black swirling cloud above roils with frantic energy. It needs a host. It needs me. But that's not going to happen. Not again.

I step toward Ninnis, ready to fight him with the last strength that I have.

Strike unfurls in his right hand, glinting in the fire light.

But when he shouts his battle cry and swings the sword, he is not aiming at me.

A second hunter has attacked! Is this a friend? One of the hunters that helped Tobias escape with Em and Luca?

The man meets a quick end at the tip of Strike. The sword pierces the attacker's heart and emerges from his back. Before I can fully grasp the turn of events, Ninnis yanks the sword from the first hunter's chest, ducks a thrown spear and swings Strike in a wide arc. Two more hunters, a man and a woman, lose their legs. The scene is horrid. Unlike anything I've seen before. People killing people without a second thought. Without hesitation.

And for what?

I no longer believe the attackers are on my side. Their lack of strategy and cunning is closer to frenzy than sacrifice. They're not thinking. They're—

A wet slurp interrupts my thoughts. Another hunter has fallen.

Shouting voices thunder around me as the army breaks into chaos. The warriors sound angry. The hunters, desperate. The others are drowned out by the sounds of battle. I look around. Hunters charge toward the circle, but they're hacking at each other as they run. It's every man for himself. And not one of them is looking at me.

Then I remember the envy in the other hunters' eyes on the day I consumed the flesh of Nephil. Each one of them craved it for themselves. And now, seeing it again coupled with the presence of Nephil himself, the hunters are slaughtering each other for the chance to be the new vessel.

Through the crowd of running, falling, and dying hunters I see Luca gripped in the arms of Kainda. His limbs hang limp. Dead or unconscious, there is no way to know. But she has not left the boy to claim the body of Nephil, which I believe she could do. If anyone could defeat Ninnis, it would be her. Is it her sense of duty that has rooted her in place? Or something else? After all , Preeg and Pyke have not left their posts either, but they stare as the scene like hungry lions. It's likely that the only thing keeping them in place is the knowledge that they wouldn't make it past Kainda and even if they did, they could never stand against Ninnis, who is now surrounded by the bodies of his fellow hunters.

Preeg suddenly grasps her throat and falls. The sudden motion turns Pyke around, but he's too slow. Em is there! She throws a knife that catches him in the chest. He falls to the ground.

Kainda spins around, facing Em, who has two blades at the ready.

The situation is precarious. Em could throw the knives accurately, but Kainda is fast and might position Luca's body in the way. Kainda could also use Luca as bait, drawing Em in close enough to strike her down with the giant hammer.

But neither move.

A man falls away from Ninnis, his throat slit. He tumbles back toward me. I roll to the side, avoiding his falling body. But I freeze again, turning my attention back to Luca and Em.

Neither woman has struck. In fact, they appear to be talking. Then I see surprise register on Em's face. I know my expression must look similar, because Kainda then hands the boy over to Em, who slings him over her shoulder. The pair duck into the shadows and flee together.

Luca is saved.

Em has escaped.

And Kainda…she has been redeemed.

A clang of metal on metal draws my attention back to the fight. A body falls. Ninnis stands in the middle of a ring of death. The hunters still alive are too busy fighting each other to stop what happens next. When I try to run at him and stumble back down to my knees, I know that I am too weak.

Ninnis grins at me. With a twitch of his hand, Strike rolls up. He attaches the weapon to his belt and then crouches. When he stands again, he clutches the body of Nephil in his hand.

Without a word or second thought, he puts the gelatinous purple mass into his mouth and swallows.

A high pitched squeal explodes from Ninnis's mouth as a violent shaking rises up from his feet and quickly claims the rest of his body. He falls, clutched by the seizure, and disappears within the circle of bodies.

I push myself to my feet, bracing myself with Whipsnap. I see Ninnis shaking, his mouth covered in white foam. *I should kill him*, I think. And end this. But I can't do it. I swore to never take a human life, even one as corrupt as Ninnis. But even if I had tried, it would be too late. The swirling black spirit of Nephil descends like a tornado. It touches down on Ninnis and enters him. The shaking stops, but he does not move.

Has the merger killed him?

No, I think, as I see his chest rising and falling from each breath. He is simply unconscious.

Kill him! Ull is free and shouting to be heard. But he has not yet realized what I have. Nephil's body has been consumed. The spirit has entered Ninnis. He is the Lord of the Nephilim, at least for now, and I am the enemy.

The fighting around me has stopped. The surviving hunters stare at me. As do the thousands of Nephilim watching the scene play out with rapt attention.

"Take him," Enki says, pointing at me.

They still need me, I realize. Ninnis will not be able to contain the spirit of Nephil forever. I am uniquely suited to the task—if only they could break me again. *They cannot break us!* Ull shouts at me.

When a buzzing sound fills my mind, I realize there is another option that I hadn't yet considered. If they can't break me, they can erase my mind, or at least control it. I feel the probing minds of a hundred gatherers trying to penetrate my thoughts.

I stagger back as more hunters emerge from the wall of Nephilim giants. Fifty. One hundred.

Even at full strength, I could not hold out long against this many hunters.

A sharp bark echoes in the tunnel.

And then chaos returns with a flash of green and red. Twelve cresties pour out of a nearby side tunnel and tear into the distracted hunters. But the attack also spurs the army into action. Some of the hunters counter attack. The rest, come for me.

Ninnis groans behind me, coming to.

I hobble around him, running away from the hunters, but there is nowhere to go. The army is behind me. The gates to Tartarus—a land of eternal suffering—stand open before me. I am trapped.

I turn to face my attackers.

Three hunters lead the charge, weapons raised. They will reach me within seconds.

I glance to the left. There is no sign of Luca, Em or Kainda. They've made it out.

The cresties continue fighting, but the tide is turning against them. They are severely outnumbered and when the Nephilim join the fight, the dinosaurs are outsized. I see a number of them quickly fall, heads crushed, bodies impaled. A slaughter. Realizing the battle is lost, Grumpy lets out a bark, and the five remaining pack members retreat, heading in the same direction as Em, Luca and Kainda, perhaps following the familiar scent.

I've been abandoned, but I am glad for it. If the cresties follow Em, they will all be safer.

I, on the other hand, am doomed.

The three hunters shout as they lunge.

I thrust my arms out, sending a gust of wind against them and fling them into some of the other charging hunters. The pack slows, keeping a safe distance. They no doubt thought my extraordinary abilities would fade when the body of Nephil left me.

With the gates of Tartarus just thirty feet behind me, the semi circle of hunters tightens. There is nowhere to run. And if they knew how weak I felt, they would have attacked already.

Enki, Enlil, Thor and Osiris join the ring.

"You are stronger than we ever imagined, Ull," Enki says.

"I am not Ull!" I shout back.

Enki chuckles. "This is the role you were born for. You are the vessel of Nephil, and you will accept him."

The buzzing in my head grows intense. I can feel my will being shattered from within. I grit my teeth and fight against it, but I am not alone.

You must run, Xin says. He sounds weak. Beaten. And I realize that the only reason the gatherers have yet to claim my mind is because he is shielding me, and feeling the majority of their attack.

A crazed scream rips through the chamber.

Heads turn and the wall of hunters parts. Ninnis steps forward. His body looks stronger. Younger. His arm is healed.

Nephil has found a host in Ninnis, if only temporarily.

Run! Xin insists.

Where? I think.

Ninnis walks toward me, confident and radiating power. He says nothing, but his unblinking eyes never waver from mine.

Pain throbs in my head.

I need an escape route. I need a distraction.

I need Behemoth.

Focusing beyond Ninnis, beyond the wall of hunters and the army of Nephilim, I feel the air surrounding the wall of fire. I return my thoughts to the molecules of oxygen, the same way I did when I made the wall flare. But this time, instead of pulling the oxygen into the flame, I draw it away.

When the light in the chamber drops by seventy percent, I know I've succeeded. As does everyone else. There is a shift of attention in the chamber as nearly everyone cranes their heads toward the extinguished wall.

Behemoth bellows with a hungry rage. The meal set out before him is unlike anything he's seen before. His thundering footsteps shake the chamber and something I never thought I'd see takes place. The Nephilim—this horde of half demon monsters conspiring to exterminate and enslave the human race—panics.

The buzzing in my head fades. The gatherers, and Xin, are gone.

The majority of hunters surrounding me break ranks and run.

But not everyone runs. Enki remains. As do the other ancient kings. They stand among Lord Nephil now and flight is not possible.

And Ninnis. He doesn't show any reaction to Behemoth's approach. He continues his calm walk toward me. I look into his eyes and sense the power there. Even with Behemoth's distraction, I will not be able to escape. Ninnis on his own would be a challenge, but he's now powered by the body and spirit of Nephil.

With the last of my strength, I direct the wind at him, hoping to knock him back and give me a moment to run—if my legs can still manage it. But he walks through the gust as though it's a gentle breeze.

"You cannot run," Ninnis says, his voice more sinister than ever before.

I step away, matching his pace in reverse so that there is a constant ten feet between us.

"And you cannot live." Ninnis unfurls Strike at his side.

Cannot live?

But they need me alive.

Nephil wouldn't—

This *isn't* Nephil!

Ninnis contains all of the power and strength of Nephil, as well as the allegiance of the Nephilim, but he has retained control of his body and mind. And to keep it that way, he needs me dead.

He sees the realization in my eyes and smiles. "Little Solomon, you never were strong enough to claim this power as your own."

He feints a thrust and I jump back.

I look behind me. The depressing darkness of Tartarus is just five feet away.

If Ninnis kills me, he wins. The Nephilim win. I cannot let that happen.

I take a step back and ready my weapon.

Ninnis laughs. "You are weak, boy. You pose no threat to me now."

"I know," I say, "But I will not let you kill me."

"You have no choice."

"There is always a choice," I say. It's a lesson I wish every hunter in the underworld would learn. To punctuate my statement, I take another step back.

Surprise registers on Ninnis's face. "You wouldn't."

I take another step. I can feel the darkness tingling around me.

"Why?" He asks.

For some reason, I think him not knowing will eat him up inside, so I simply say, "I hope you figure it out someday. Goodbye, Ninnis."

I see his face contort with confusion as I take one more step back.

Then I see nothing.

The darkness has swallowed me.

And in an instant I realize I've made a mistake.

I've never felt such sadness. Such loneliness. Even the voice of Ull is gone once again.

I step forward, hoping to stand before Ninnis again. I would prefer a thousand deaths to the sorrow that consumes me. I try to gather my thoughts. I'm still me. My mind is still intact. But when a shiver wracks my body, I realize just how helpless I have become.

I can no longer feel the land, water and air. This realm is physical, but somehow separate from Antarctica. And for the first time since setting foot on the continent of my birth, I feel...

Cold.

EPILOGUE

Lieutenant Ninnis felt proud once more. After a lifetime of servitude and submission he had finally proved his worth. As a man. As a hunter. And now, as Lord of the Nephilim. While Nephil had not fully bonded to him, mind and spirit, he contained all of the power and desires of the ancient demon.

Except for one. Nephil still wanted the boy. Solomon. Only then could Nephil be fully in control. And while Ninnis served the Nephilim with all of his being, he did not want to give up this power.

He could feel it burning inside him, rotting him from the inside even as he grew stronger. But he believed it would be better to burn bright, like a star, for a moment than to remain in the shadows. He would lead the Nephilim to the surface. He would wage war on humanity. And he would instill a new era of Nephilim rule on this planet.

Having completed all of that, his death, and Nephil's, would be acceptable to him. Though he knew the ancient being, whose spirit wouldn't carry on in death, disagreed. That said, there was also no choice. The boy was gone. Far from their reach in the realm of Tartarus.

Ninnis frowned as he remembered Solomon's final act. His willingness to not just die, but endure eternal torture rather than give himself over to his enemies, revealed a strength Ninnis did not believe possible. He'd been wrong about the boy. He wasn't just strong enough to contain the spirit of Nephil, he'd been strong enough to repel it.

Pain gripped Ninnis's chest. He rubbed his hand over the spot, thinking of Solomon's face disappearing in the dark grip of Tartarus. It was a sacrifice he could not comprehend. His thoughts drifted to the message Solomon had once carved in a wall. 'I forgive you.' He'd thought the words hollow. Left to taunt him. To make him feel weak.

But now? The boy's convictions proved real.

And were he not confined in Tartarus, Solomon might actually be a threat. His power wasn't simply physical, it was also transformative.

In the aftermath of Solomon's departure, Ninnis had ordered a census. Behemoth had devoured hundreds. The dinosaurs killed another thirty. Ninnis himself had slain twenty-five before claiming the flesh of Nephil. He wanted to know the state of their forces before the battle was waged. What he discovered was surprising, not because of how many were dead, but because of how many had deserted. Thirty-six hunters were missing, including his daughter, Kainda. He couldn't be sure they'd all turned against the Nephilim, but it was possible some, inspired by the boy's sacrifice, found some part of themselves that had been buried since their breaking.

If that spread, if all the hunters were won over, a war would need to be fought here on Antarctica before they could move to the outside world.

But that would never happen. With the boy gone, his influence would never spread.

A hot wind surged past Ninnis. He turned his eyes up, looking at the bright sun which now hung in the sky for so long.

When he bonded with Nephil, he became aware of everything the demon had experienced, including his battle for control of the boy—a battle that identified at least one traitor—Xin, who had thus far eluded capture. But he also recalled the very first moments of the bonding, when Nephil's spirit nearly took full control of Solomon. As he realized the host was not willing, he reached out and grasped the land, the whole Earth, and wrenched it free from its moorings. It was the opening salvo of their assault on the surface—a first strike that had already claimed countless lives.

Ninnis smiled as he looked at the scene around him. He stood atop a mountain that just a month ago was covered in snow, but which now held the first signs of green growth. The Earth's crust had shifted. Antarctica had been relocated to the equator. From his perch, he watched rivers of melt water flow into the ocean. Far in the distance, he could see giant ice shelves floating away. They had reshaped the world and made the Nephilim's home a paradise once again. And the land became fertile, spurred on by the healing properties of Nephilim blood spilled into the earth. But that wasn't all. The continent was expanding. Growing. With trillions upon trillions of tons of ice flowing away, the massive weight pushing the continent deeper below sea level had lifted.

Ninnis let out a laugh that rolled down the mountainside and over the exposed citadel of Olympus.

Antarktos was rising.

ABOUT THE AUTHOR

JEREMY ROBINSON is the author of ten thrillers including *Instinct* and *Threshold*, the second two books in his exciting Jack Sigler series. His novels have been translated into nine languages. He is also the director of New Hampshire AuthorFest, a non-profit organization promoting literacy in New Hampshire where he lives with his wife and three children.

Connect with Robinson online:
www.jeremyrobinsononline.com

COMING WINTER 2011

THE LAST HUNTER

ASCENT

BOOK III OF THE ANTARKTOS SAGA

TO STAY INFORMED VISIT
WWW.JEREMYROBINSONONLINE.COM AND
SIGN UP FOR THE NEWSLETTER

CPSIA information can be obtained at www.ICGtesting.com
Printed in the USA
237805LV00004B/1/P